Adventures of the Amethyst Dragon

DRAGON SPEAKER CHRONICLES

JULIE L. KRAMER

Copyright © 2023 by Julie L. Kramer

All rights reserved.

No part of this book may be reproduced in any form or by any electronic or mechanical means, including information storage and retrieval systems, without written permission from the author, except for the use of brief quotations in a book review.

Cover Design by Carol Marques Designs

Chapter One

The egg rocked gently in place like a crying child. The amethyst surface was smooth and without blemish, at least for the moment, although the fact that it was moving was evidence enough that it wouldn't be long before the state of the exterior of the egg changed. The torch on the wall cast flickering shadows on the egg, turning the shell translucent. A dark form was visible as if lit from the inside out. It had a tail and wings and a head, but that was pretty much all that was visible through the shell. There was probably more to it, at least if past knowledge served, but seeing it through the shell was no way to confirm that. As of now, it was merely a strange creature that had not yet made itself known to the world.

  A silver haired woman touched the rocking egg as if to comfort it. The rocking slowed for a moment, then increased in speed and intensity, like a child eager to ask questions of a trusted adult but knowing that there was a task to finish first. The elderly woman's back was hunched as she placed both her wizened hands on the egg, stroking it gently as she knelt, knees cracking painfully with each inch she drew closer to the floor. Her full lips parted as a radiant smile lit her wrinkled features. Her eyes were pale purple, just like the orb, shimmering in the darkness. Her violet eyes and silver hair marked her as a Dragon Speaker, one that could speak to dragons and understand what they felt, although that was not all that she was. Not all Dragon Speakers had those same hallmarks, although most of them did. While she had some of the same hallmarks as the other Speakers did, this woman was special.

She was the only one of her kind, chosen to look out for the purple dragons, which were a gift for humanity. There were several different colors and types of dragons that lived in the wild or happily coexisted with people, anything from darkest black to palest blue, but the purple dragons were different. There were no wild purple dragons, and there was a reason for that.

Whereas dragons in the wild hatched because of the situation around them, or rather hatched if there was even slightly enough heat for them to draw on to accomplish the breaking of their shell, purple dragons were hatched for a specific person. That was the bargain that had been made so long ago, that the purple dragons, the weakest of their species, would be paired with humans. It had been done to ensure that dragons and humans fought no longer, but few knew of that. Few know of the dragons at all, and none knew of the woman who watched over them.

The woman was part of an order of the seers of the future, those who could see the people that would influence it and did their best to make things happen the way that they were meant to. In this particular case, two purple dragons would need to be hatched, a bonded pair to go with the young man and the woman who would one day fall in love, and that was a challenge that she was more than willing to undertake. It would be better to start with the female of the pair, since females required more heat to hatch and stay healthy. Strange, since the females were the ones that couldn't breathe flames, but that didn't matter. She was destined to do great things along with her silver haired rider, even if she couldn't breathe fire. Things would work out as they were meant to.

The egg the woman cradled was only one of many in the room. They were all colored in various shades of purple, from deep amethyst to pale lavender. Each was nestled deep in its own bed of rags, resting on shelves carved into the stone walls of the cave. Ridged grooves kept the eggs in place. Flickering torches in iron brackets illuminated the eggs; a nest of equally ratty blankets marked where the woman slept. Purple dragons weren't the only ones that could bond with Dragon Speakers, but they were the only ones that required a human touch in order to hatch. With every other type of dragon, blue and green and red and so on, the dragons would hatch without any interference. It was a long process for a purple dragon to be hatched, which was why they were so rare and so special. Purple dragons were also the only ones who abandoned their young as soon as they were laid, which had been the original reason for choosing them to bond with humans in the first place. It had been hundreds of years, but purple dragons were still working their way into being trusted by the humans with the help of their Speakers. And that help started with the woman in the cave.

Despite the late hour, the woman seemed too focused on the egg to even consider sleep, and it was easy to see why. Its surface was riddled with cracks as the creature within prepared to make her grand entrance into the world, and the woman's lavender eyes stared with avid interest. The fissures in the polished surface of the egg widened, and the woman startled violently as a tiny head erupted, showering egg shards to the stone floor. The woman's giggle rang out and the hatchling tilted its purple head, blinking amber eyes. She scooped up the creature, trilling gently with her tongue. Young dragons like this were always a bit shy and unsure of themselves, so the sooner she started building up this little creature's confidence, the better. One of the advantages of sending a purple dragon to bond with someone, especially a youth like the girl with silver hair, was that they were a blank slate, a pond without a ripple. Rather than trying to train a dragon that had been wild its entire life, the girl would have a dragon that had literally been born for her. The two were fated to be companions, and it was always exciting to begin the process. Today, that started with showing the young dragon the girl that she would be spending the rest of her life with.

The Speaker carried the dragon into the center of the cave where a deep pool of milky white liquid rippled gently; it made no sense, since there was no breeze to ruffle it or disturb the serenity of the hidden cave, but the woman had long ago given up trying to question it. The tiny dragon crawled to the edge of the liquid, webbed wings outspread for balance but still a quick shuffle despite her ungainly appearance. It wouldn't take long for her to grow into her body, since dragons were born with everything they needed to go out into the world. Technically the tiny female could have flown away right now, although that would not be something that the woman would advise; purple dragons were naturally smaller and weaker than the other dragons, so she would need all of her strength when it came time to find her Speaker.

Silver claws at the ends of her wings gouged into the soft sand as she crawled forward, using the claws for balance the same way a person would use their toes.

Images swirled on the surface of the pool. Young people, none more than nineteen years of age. Some male, some female. The dragon's amber eyes stared at the water, watching the images flash by like darting fish that she could not catch, faster and faster before they slammed to a halt on a specific person. The dragon sighed softly, the flicking of her tail slowing as she hummed softly.

Some part of her knew that this was the other half of her heart, the girl that she had literally been born to bond with. It had never occurred to the woman to be ashamed of bringing a creature into the world specifically because of the things that she would do one day; none of the dragons had ever expressed any discontent with the Speaker that they had been chosen to bond with and as far as she knew, she had never made a mistake while working with the pairs.

Even now, still wet from the egg, the tiny dragon knew that she and the girl were meant for another, and she was practically vibrating with the need to reach her, as if she could wade into the milky liquid and be at her side in a matter of moments. If only that were so.

The image was of a girl, silver haired like an old maid though she couldn't have been more than fifteen. She was tall and lean, built like she would grow still more. Her eyes were palest purple, a shade darker than the young dragon's scales.

"She's a good one," the old woman approved, stroking

the tiny dragon's back. Like all dragons of her type, she was built like a racing dog, lean and thin. Rising from her place in the sand, the matron retrieved a map and a purple crystal on a slender silver chain. She spread the map on the short wooden table, weighting the corners with stones so that the edges of the aged parchment didn't roll; she was gentle as she placed the stones, because this map was so ancient that even the slightest of movements could have shredded the thin parchment, nearly translucent with age in the candlelight. The crystal began to spin, the silver chain held loosely between her thumb and pointer finger. Her wrist flexed as it spun slowly. The crystal thumped to a halt on the map and the woman leaned closer to study the location. A tiny island that was hardly befitting a young woman that would end up being as important as this one, but so be it.

"Look, little one." The tiny dragon pounced onto the table, disturbing cups, coins, and other curiosities with her tail as she snuffled on the map with her slender muzzle. "This is where we'll find your Speaker." The tiny dragon chimed gently, and they both turned back to the pool to watch the girl. Only they two knew how quickly, and drastically, her life was about to change. For the better, or for the worse, was entirely her choice.

Chapter Two

"Whoo!" I yelled as Iona's wings beat and the freezing air rushed past my face, then choked as a lock of my thick silver hair smacked me in the mouth, stubbornly refusing to return to its proper place as I struggled to peel it from my tongue.

At full flight speed, it was both a surprise and surprisingly gross.

Still, I would prefer my own hair to being pelted with bugs, which was possible but not uncommon. A pair of goggles were tucked in the saddlebags behind me, but what I needed more was the band to keep my hair in place; besides, I hated to wear the goggles. They squeezed my head and left red markings on my face when I wore them for too long.

The majority of my hair was already braided, but the

majority wasn't the problem; it was the tiny little wisps that brushed my forehead and cheeks. Those were the ones I had to worry about, since they stubbornly refused to stay where they were supposed to. I had never viewed having thick hair as a curse until I had started riding a dragon, when it went from a cause for celebration to an absolute nuisance. I only had a few options to keep my hair where it was supposed to be, and none of them were that great. For one thing, there was only so much that a slender leather band on my forehead could do in the face of so much hair. The only other option was to wear the helmet that I had made for myself, and I was even less enthusiastic about that one. It was hot and that felt like it was squeezing my head just as much as the goggles did, probably because I had made it a few years ago. It still fit well enough to do in a pinch, but I hated wearing it, and I tried to avoid it if at all possible.

The dragon I rode rumbled her version of a laugh, amethyst scales vibrating against my thighs with her mirth. I finally managed to peel the hair away, tucking it into my braid so that I could lean forward in my saddle. The straps that attached me to the saddle shifted, iron rings clinking. The straps were necessary, for both my safety and Iona's. It wasn't that I wasn't capable of riding a dragon well, because I considered myself at the very least a competent rider, if not a bit better. Unfortunately, my dragon took great joy in pulling dangerous stunts when I wasn't paying attention. After the first few times she had decided that she was angry and let me free fall until I was sure that I was going to die, I had decided to add the straps as a safety precaution. They weren't the only modifications that I had made, but they were the most important. If I really had to think about it, I would have said that they were more for my safety than hers, but she would be just as upset as I was if I fell out of the saddle and died. Or, at least, I hoped so, although times like this made me question that.

"I'm glad you think it's funny," I grumbled, but I couldn't help the reluctant grin that made one side of my mouth kink upward; it wouldn't hurt anything, especially since she couldn't see it, and besides, it wasn't a big enough deal that I was going to be upset about it. The two of us were pretty much the only interaction that we ever had with a living creature that we weren't going to eat, so there was no room for any kind of anger between us. And besides, I could feel through the bond that she had meant no harm, so I couldn't bring myself to be angry with her.

Another rumble as she writhed back and forth in midair, as if she were shaking with laughter. It was a human mannerism that she had learned from the village drunk, of all people, when she had spent her days silently watching over me as I went through my daily life in the village. I hadn't known about it then, hadn't known that she was watching or even that she was nearby until she had fought a massive dragon and I had done my very best to nurse her back to health; I still didn't know how long she had been hanging around the village before she had finally revealed herself to me, and I didn't think that I ever would.

Frustrated with the tiny silver hairs battering my face with every beat of Iona's wings, I loosened the straps around my legs and everything else that held me to the saddle, planting my feet and tightening my core so that I could stand up on her back. Iona was not a terribly large dragon, but it was still necessary to stand if I wanted to reach the saddlebags. Even if she had been much smaller, I still wouldn't have been able to reach the rear of the saddle, because as flexible as I was, I would not be able to twist my entire body around so much that I could face almost entirely in the opposite direction while still having my legs strapped to the saddle; it was not physically possible, and even if it had been, it would have been immensely painful.

The position of the saddle changed day by day, depending on what we were doing. That was the easiest way I had found to ensure that neither of us were sore from the saddle, as well as the fact that we would never grow bored of a routine, most likely because there never was one for us to grow irritated with.

If we were going somewhere we knew, or rather keeping to a path both of us knew well, then the saddle was as it was now, practically against her neck with the straps around the base of her throat as short as the rings could make them. It meant that it would be slow going, with me in a position that would be better for comfort for both of us, although it might grow tiresome for her if I stayed that way for too long. If it was going to be a long trip, the saddle went behind her wings, allowing me to stretch out across her back to more evenly distribute my weight. With her saddle so far forward, I had to completely leave it and walk across her cool scales, my toes clenching in my boots to keep from sliding from the slick surface.

I would have felt much better if I had been able to take my boots off and walk completely across her back, since bare feet were better to balance with than boots would ever be, but I highly doubted I would ever get my boots back if they fell off at this height, and I quite liked my boots; I was also not particularly keen on walking around with nothing to protect my feet until I could figure out how to either buy or make a new pair. Besides, Iona was not always the most willing to dive after me when I fell off, or rather, she made *sure* I fell off. I had serious doubts that she would even try to save my boots if it came down to it, so I wasn't willing to take the risk.

I sat on her hindquarters in an ungainly slide as a particularly strong beat of her wings knocked my feet out from under me, wrapping my legs around her tail to stay in place while I leaned over to loosen the buckles and reach into the saddlebags. Such stunts were not uncommon for the two of us, but that didn't mean that there wasn't a solid moment of panic for me when I felt my feet leave her back and the empty air under me; logically I knew that she wouldn't let me fall to my death, because the bond between us was entirely too strong for her to remain unaffected if such a terrible thing occurred, but that didn't mean that I was fond of the feeling of floating weightless in the frigid air and wondering if today was the the day that Iona was finally too slow to save me from myself and it all ended.

Still, I tried to focus on the task at hand, because allowing my thoughts to linger on the worst that could happen was not going to prove productive, nor was it going to help the slow sense of anxiety currently bouncing back and forth through the bond between us.

I flipped my hair out of my face, contemplating taking my hair down to braid it more firmly before realizing that that was quite possibly the worst thing that I could do; there would be no controlling it at this height, and I highly doubted that I would be able to pull it out of my face at all at this height and speed. I was not about to risk that, especially since Iona wasn't the type that would land and allow me to get it back in place.

She didn't have any hair, so she didn't really understand what a nuisance it could be for me to have to deal with it, nor the fact that it could entirely close off my vision. The band for my hair was tossed on the top from where I had thrown it last night, and I was grateful I wouldn't have to dig for it. I plucked it off the pile and slid it into place, tucking the loose strands into the leather and enjoying the sudden clarity of sight. Now the interesting part was going to be keeping it that way while I got back to the saddle. I wasn't worried about the band falling out, because it was snug enough that I could feel it pressing against my forehead, although not enough that it was causing me pain; I was more worried about whether or not I could stay upright and not fall on my face while I tried to get back to the only place on Iona's back where I actually felt safe, which was in the saddle.

Rather than standing and risking the same danger that my slight tumble had reminded me of before, I crawled on my hands and knees back to the saddle, swinging my legs forward to slide in. It wasn't exactly comfortable, since it would be a neat trick to make something out of a few thin layers of leather that actually made letting your body rub up against hard scales all day comfortable. I had made a few reminders for myself that I needed to find some way to add more padding to at least the seat of the saddle, but that was yet another item on the long list of things that I wanted to do that had yet to be accomplished.

The dampness from the clouds around us threatened to soak my skin and hair, but it had no chance against my armor. Heavy, stiffened black leather hugged my chest, covered with purple scales that my dragon had once shed; pads jutted from my shoulders and lay flat against my upper arms, held in place by a strap around my bicep. Long sleeves of the same black leather protected my arms, randomly dotted with more of the same tiny scales. I added the scales as Iona shed them; eventually both arms would be entirely covered by scales, assuming that my sewing skills allowed me to continue wearing the armor that long. A black ring wrapped around each of my middle fingers to hold the suit in place, which I was constantly fiddling with whenever I was anxious. A deep purple dragon was painted on the silver shoulder pads, a design that I had created with much trial and error, which was the full extent of my artistic abilities. I wore short black boots that were tight to my calves and fitted black pants, also arrayed in glittering scales. I had made the outfit myself, but I was constantly trying to improve it. My latest improvement had been to add a sort of wings to the suit, based on Iona's wings, although mine were black instead of purple. There were still a few tweaks to be made. And by tweaks, I meant the wings had yet to be anything other than a nuisance. At best they were a decoration, but it was likely that I would remove them and tuck them away until I could figure out a way to make them work better.

They would become just another failed invention in a

long line of my curiosities. At the moment their most important job was to provide a sense of entertainment for Iona, since she seemed to think that me having the wings on my clothing was a challenge for her to make me fall off and "fly" on my own even more often than she ever had before. If ever there had been a reason to take them off, this was it.

"I'm hungry," I said finally, willing to let it go.

Another rumble, this one of agreement. Both of our stomachs were growling loudly enough to be audible even over the rush of air with each beat of Iona's wings. My sense of hunger was doubled by Iona's own, a ghost sensation of emptiness in my stomach that was more than what I could have felt on my own. It made it almost dizzyingly painful, or at least enough of an ache that I was half-tempted to turn around and sneak some food from the saddlebags, although I almost immediately changed my mind and faced forward again, shaking my head as if I could rid myself of the thought. I had always promised myself that I would never eat or drink if Iona couldn't, which included if she couldn't because she was just flying. This was not the perfect occasion to break the vow that I had made to myself long ago and every day since, if there even was such a thing. I could wait, and wait I would.

Below us, the ocean rippled slowly as far as the eye could see in any direction, broken only by a small island that was like a dot of green in the middle of a tartan cloth.

The sight was beautiful, but it was also somewhat depressing. That meant that there was nowhere for us to land if we needed to, save for that island, and no help if something happened. While I enjoyed my privacy as much as the next girl, especially since so many people had taken it upon themselves to share their opinion on why I was a terrible dragon rider or a terrible person because I was a terrible person or some combination thereof. Still, enjoying privacy and wanting to feel like I was the only person left in the entire world were two completely different things.

Upon closer inspection of the island, I realized that it was really more like a tower of stone jutting from the deep indigo waters of the ocean. Lush green grass covered the entire surface, which looked very welcoming considering that we had been flying for hours and my only break, however brief it may have been, had been to grab my hair band; that was hardly enough to relieve hours of pins and needles, unless I counted the brief moment of fearing for my life as a bit of added incentive, which I did not.

The island was a welcoming sight, and apparently I wasn't the only one who thought so. Occasionally Iona decided to ignore the islands and continue flying, but that was not the case here. For one thing, I was sure that she was just as ready to feel solid ground beneath our feet again, even if she hadn't said so or even complained about being exhausted; I could feel the impending weakness through the bond, and although I prepared myself to have to fight to make her land, hopefully it would be more of a strongly worded argument than an actual fight. And for another thing, there was no telling when we would find another place to land, so it wouldn't exactly make sense for us not to take advantage of every opportunity that we could.

Iona agreed, because her claws extended as she approached, wings flaring back as she landed with her hind legs touching the ground first. Her claws retracted as soon as they touched the grass; her claws were surprisingly delicate, and they could and would tear if she turned wrong on them. Her webbed amethyst wings trembled with exhaustion. Ever graceful, she flopped bonelessly onto her stomach with a solid *thump*. I was still hooked to the saddle, and my knees ground painfully into the grass as she writhed, trying to make herself comfortable.

I fumbled to free myself, my exhausted hands struggling to release my clip from its hook. I lifted my right leg over her back; Iona did her part to help me dismount by rolling sideways, dumping me over her wing and onto the hard ground.

I sat up indignantly. "Thanks for that."

She snaked her long neck toward me, opening her mouth to reveal massive white fangs. It was her smile, or at least as close to it as she could manage. Dragons learned from their riders; with her naturally sunny, if mischievous disposition, it hadn't taken her long to pick up on the habit. Just like it hadn't taken long for her to laugh. Her laugh was really just a quiet, high pitched growl in an attempt to emulate a human's mirth. Her laughter rippled in my bones, and I grinned slowly.

We were both exhausted.

This tiny hunk of rock didn't have any shelter, but at this point, that might not even matter. At this point I could have slept outside in the rain and counted myself lucky, but that wasn't counting the partial shelter I'd had when I slept under Iona's wings.

Iona sprawled on her stomach with her long neck extended. A feeling drifted from her more strongly this time, and it was certainly one I agreed with.

"Yes, I'm hungry too," I said aloud. My stomach growled in confirmation.

I climbed over Iona's wings as she shifted, grumbling. A satchel hung from the rear of the saddle, the thick tan fabric emblazoned with the purple dragon on my upper arm. Iron rings dangled also, in case I had to hook something to the saddle. I unbuckled the satchel and dug inside, using the sensitive tips of my fingers to feel for what I was seeking. I came up with a skin of fresh water and took a swig before I continued. Iona could drink water directly from any water source, even the ocean, which was what she would likely do once she roused herself. She had glands on the interior of her throat that filtered out toxins and anything else that would make the water undrinkable.

There. Of course what I was looking for would be at the very bottom of the satchel. It was a carefully wrapped pouch, tied tightly at the top with a leather thong. I untied it and opened the top of the bag, taking a bite of the dried jerky as I dug once more. This jerky was pretty much the only food that I had that I ate consistently during my travels. I never knew if there would be food to eat where we traveled, or if any food would be safe to eat; I'd had a bad experience with poisonous berries more than once.

Iona peeled herself off the grass, wings ruffling. I took the hint and removed her saddle, unbuckling it so that it could drop to the ground next to me. The curved black leather was thin but thick enough to be comfortable for long distances. The largest buckle was under her belly; another was at the back of her neck, with the strap wrapped around her neck like a collar. I had made the saddle myself, and that extra collar meant for additional stability because without it, the saddle tended to flip upside down if she maneuvered too quickly. With me still attached. The collar also spread my weight evenly. The next time I found an island with the supplies I needed, I was going to add more straps, but I had not had the time or the materials yet.

I had been forced to make the saddle myself because of

how different Iona was from other dragons, not just in mind but in body. There were plenty of dragons at home, but they were all varying shades of blue, from the palest turquoise to such a dark navy as to be almost black. There was an uneasy alliance between them and my people. The dragons helped with our largest tasks, like ferrying stones or building ships, and in return we provided them with all the food they wanted. I had it on good authority that the dragons didn't like humans, and I knew the humans didn't trust the dragons. Most of the time it was uncertain whether or not the dragons would show up to help. This was a tenuous arrangement at best, and someday soon it would blow up in our faces if we didn't do something to mend the relationship.

Iona was very different. For one thing, she wasn't blue as the other dragons were, but rather a deep amethyst purple. Threads of silver shot through the veins in her wings. Her tail was long and slender. Her silver-webbed wings were wide and webbed, like a bat's. Unlike the dragons at home, there were no claws on the edges of her wings. There were no spikes on her neck and back. Her teeth were long and sharp, but they lacked the two distinctive fangs of the dragons where I had grown up. The blue dragons could breathe flame, whereas Iona could only shoot bursts of light; they were blinding, yes, but there was no heat.

She was as capable of defending herself as any dragon was, but Iona was built for flight, not fighting.

Once the saddle was removed, she roused herself. She flung herself over the side of the rock in a streak of purple and silver. I rushed to the edge, staring down after her. Her wings streamed back, then pinned tightly to her sides as she plunged into the water, head first. I smirked.

It took a moment before she resurfaced with her tail slapping the water as she writhed like a playful puppy. She was fishing. And I wasn't going to begrudge her a little playtime if she had the energy.

While Iona was swimming, I removed a thin piece of paper from my armor and spread it carefully on the grass. I had once carried it in my saddlebags, but they had been stolen too many times for me to be comfortable with that any longer; now I carried it tucked in my armor, in a special pocket on my upper arm, hidden under the piece on my shoulders.

Dark shapes were sketched onto the paper, some of the ink faded with age and some still dark. I withdrew a small stick from my pack, careful to keep the end pointed away from my fingers. This was another invention that I had come up with. It was a stick that I had hollowed out, with a vial of black ink nestled inside. A hairline crack at the bottom allowed a thin stream of ink to escape when the point was facing downward. When it was in my saddlebags, it was kept in a special container so that the point was always facing upward and the ink couldn't escape. I had an idea that if I could somehow cap it and add a sensor or a trigger so that the ink would only release if I put pressure on it, but I hadn't had time to work on my theory yet.

This map was my purpose in life. I had always been a strange child. I had always been in awe of the majesty of the dragons, but something felt off with the giant blue beasts. That changed when I bonded with Iona, and discovered that I was a dragon rider, one of the few humans capable of communicating with dragons. I didn't hear their thoughts; it was more like a feeling, like anger, fear, or hunger.

The hunger that had been rippling from Iona while she swam slowly diminished. I smiled, knowing that she had found the fish she sought. I sketched the day's findings on the map. Nothing too interesting, just a few towers of stone and an abandoned ship, tossed high on a massive rock. Once I finished updating the map, I withdrew a sheaf of papers, shuffled through them until I found a clean sheet, and went to work drawing the ship I had seen today. Every day I drew the most interesting thing I had seen that day from memory, and today that was the ship.

The ship had run aground many years ago, or at least as near as I could tell; it certainly hadn't been recent. The thick wood of its mast had splintered and cracked, toppling in half to the deck, which was full of gaping holes that admitted light to the hold below. The ragged, frayed material of the sails dangled forlornly in the water. The ship was still hung up on that rock, its barnacle encrusted hull trapped on the stone as if it had been impaled. I had wanted to explore the ship more, but Iona's labored wingbeats had warned me that she would not be able to lift herself into the air again if we landed on the deck, and I didn't trust that the ship wouldn't sink again with the added weight, for good this time. A small detour tomorrow wouldn't do us any harm.

I signed the completed drawing with my name, curving the letters with a flourish in the lower right corner. Asta. Water droplets dripped from Iona's wings as she heaved herself onto the grass, shaking the liquid from her glistening body. I flinched as the frigid waters splashed my face.

"Thank you for getting me wet," I said dryly, rubbing my face off on my arm. I swiped a stray drop from my cheek with the back of my hand. "Are you telling me I stink? That I need a bath, like you?"

Iona lifted one wing slowly before lowering it, the same way a human would shrug. Her hunger had abated and was replaced by quiet contentment. She padded over to investigate my drawing. She lowered her head over my shoulder to give it a sniff, and I stroked the underside of her jaw as I waited for the verdict. The scales on her underside were smaller and more tightly packed than those on her back and sides, in order to protect her more vulnerable places. It was the same on her belly.

"What do you think, girl?"

She sniffed the paper more fervently, then hummed gently in approval. She flopped onto her stomach, her wings folded loosely.

The sun was sinking, only just above the horizon. I folded up my drawing and the map, carefully tucking them into their places in my clothing. A bath didn't sound bad in theory, but there were other factors to be considered. The water was frigid. It was a decent drop to the water, close enough that I could jump without hurting myself but far enough that it would be a struggle to climb back up, especially with wet hands and feet. Iona could drop me in the water, and would happily dump me off in her current mood. The problem wasn't going down; it was coming back up. I could have tried to have her bring me back up, but she was already deeply asleep, and everyone knew that waking a sleeping dragon was a good way to get eaten.

Iona snored softly, tendrils of smoke trickling from her narrow nostrils. Her tail twitched, the scales flexing. That was another difference between her and the other dragons from home, who had spikes on their tails as well as their backs and heads. There were no spikes on her, at least not yet, which was good, because most nights I ended up flopped over her back. I *had* wanted to bathe before I slept, so that at least I wouldn't stink before we started out tomorrow, even if I would stink before the end of it. On the other hand, jumping off the smallest island I had ever been on, to bathe in frigid water in the dark and surrounded by gods knew what was in the water, and with no dragon to pick me up, did not seem like a good way to live a long life. I would have to scale the rock back up soaking wet without light to guide me and no knowledge of the rocks.

None of those things sounded remotely appealing.

"Not tonight," I decided.

Iona twitched.

Checking one last time that my saddlebags were sealed and there was no one around, I slid down against her side and watched the sun sink. Whether it went dark before I did, I didn't know.

Chapter Three

I coughed and jerked back as Iona's wing poked my face. The thin webbing had covered my nose and mouth, which was a rude awakening to say the least. I was sprawled over her neck and shoulders, my stomach across her shoulder with one wing wedged under my hip. The other wing was the one I needed to worry about. It was one thing to be woken up by something and entirely another to be woken up by something preventing you from breathing.

I slid backward onto the grass with a muffled groan. I still needed a bath, so I stripped down to my undergarments, strode to the edge of the rock, and dove, straightening my body like an arrow. What better way to wake up? Otherwise I would lay there all day, or at least until Iona started to bother me.

My fingertips shot through the wall of frigid water,

breath exploding from my lungs in a gasp. Bubbles flowing from my nose, I stroked to the surface and gasped for air as goosebumps rippled across my skin. I sank up to my shoulders in the water. The sun was hovering just above the horizon now, yellow and orange lines rippling on the water's surface. My long logs stroked in the cool water to keep me afloat. I reached up and unbound my long silver hair.

The locks were stiff with sweat and sleep, some pasted flat from wearing my helmet yesterday and some poking up from having slept on it. Scale imprints on my stomach and chest showed where I had flopped on Iona, along with my left hand, which had been pinned under her body.

When I had first bonded with Iona, we had learned to trust together. I had once slept under her wing, more for her wishes than mine. Her protective instincts told her to hold me close. That was fine for her, but waking up in complete darkness, clutched in a dragon's claws, didn't help me any. As we grew more comfortable, she learned to let go. Now I woke up sprawled across her neck most days, which might not have been the most comfortable pose but did provide me more freedom of movement than being under her wing.

I dunked my head under the water, pasting it to my head. My long fingers raked through the thick curls, winding them around my fingers to loosen the tangles. Slowly the coils loosened. I swam slowly to the base of the rock. Small shelves jutted, naturally formed in the stone.

I had placed a small pouch of oils on the lowest one only inches above the lapping water. Inside the small pouch were three short vials: one green, one blue, and one purple. I chose the purple and carefully uncorked it, dabbing a dot onto my palm and mixing it into my hair, then dipping under the water to wash it away. The oils were something else that I had discovered in my travels; not as useful as weapons or medicines, but still popular when I traded. These three were my favorites.

They weren't the only ones I had brought back.

"Iona!" I called. I could have climbed back up, but I didn't feel like breaking an arm falling back into the water. I felt bad for waking her, but I had no doubt that she would fall back asleep while I was eating the morning meal. "Iona!"

With a thunderous snarl, the dragon hurtled over the side of the sea stack and plunged into the water next to me. A wave shoved me under and I made the mistake of gasping for air, getting a mouthful of water instead; sputtering, I clawed my way to the surface and spit out the salty water, my mouth full of the briny taste.

Iona was swimming in slow circles around me with only her eyes visible, looking every inch a predator. Irritation radiated from her.

"Was that necessary?" I treaded water, craning my

neck in an attempt to keep her in view. I reached to climb onto her back and she jerked to the side, refusing to be touched; her tail splashed a wave in my direction, dousing me once more as I swiped my wet hair out of my eyes.

"Look, I'm sorry I woke you. Forgive me if I don't want to break my arm this early in the morning," I grumbled. Her irritation faded, replaced by a cooler emotion that I was just as wary of. "Iona..." I warned.

The water lurched as she lunged. I dove, but not fast enough. Her claws tightened around my bare midriff and she launched out of the water, wings showering water onto the ocean's surface as she pounded upward. She swooped over the sea stack and dumped me. I tucked and rolled, leading with my forearm and doing my best not to knee myself in the head. I sat up, swiping grass off my damp body. I wanted to be irritated that I had just gotten done washing up and was dirty already, but it wasn't her fault; I had woken her, and I didn't blame her for being upset. Besides, dirt and grass wiped off, and at least I didn't stink anymore.

"That's fair. I deserved that."

Iona snorted in agreement as she settled down to sleep, smoke trailing from her nostrils; it had always seemed strange to me, that she could produce smoke but no flame. At least, no flame yet, but it seemed that her blasts of blinding white light had been producing heat recently. Perhaps someday there would be a flame. If not, then she was still more capable of defending herself than I was.

A few fish flopped on the ground at Iona's feet. I went to the saddlebags and withdrew a large cloth, drying off quickly so that I could slip into my clothes. I gathered up the few sticks I could find and built a small fire to cook the fish.

I had my own ways of getting things done. I withdrew a small, glittering stone from my boot, then the knife strapped to the underside of my right wrist. I was left hand dominant, so the knife had to be on my right wrist in order to be within reach. It was the only thing that I carried that could be described as a weapon. I had once carried it in my boot, but now I wanted it close at hand, just in case.

Positioning the stone above the pile of sticks, I scraped the blade of the knife quickly across the rough surface; orange and yellow sparks showered onto the dry sticks. It took several tries before flame started to lick at the base of the tower. I speared one of the fish on my knife and leaned over the fire, lying back to let it cook.

Once my fish was cooked, I ate quickly. Iona roused herself and chomped down the remaining fish, rising to her feet, wings rustling in anticipation of flight. I quickly stomped out the fire and climbed onto Iona's back, settling my feet in the stirrups. They were short and molded against her sides, just wide enough for my feet.

Iron strips covered the top of my feet to keep them in place.

"So what do you want to do today?" I asked. Iona raised her head and sniffed the air, her long neck arched proudly in the breeze. "Are we going to continue south, or should we double back and explore the half sunk ship?"

Iona answered my question as she launched into the air, twirling to head back in the direction from the day before. It wasn't far back to the ship, which may have been the reason that I couldn't stop thinking about it last night; it had been fresh in my mind. She hovered slowly over the rotting boards, lowering her hind legs to see if it would hold her weight. The wood creaked alarmingly and I placed my hand on her neck to draw her attention; her head snaked back to look at me.

"I'll go myself. Just don't go far in case I need you" I swung my leg over her neck and dropped the short distance, my knees flexing in case it gave way under my weight. Iona hovered, grumbling to express the concern that radiated through our bond. The wood creaked but held, and I made a gesture to point out that everything was fine. Neither of us were fully convinced.

I padded to the hatch leading down to the cargo hold, carefully avoiding the huge gaps in the deck. The iron hatch was partially rusted away. I grasped it carefully, grabbing the smoothest piece I could find and avoiding the jagged spikes; it would be just my luck that I would cut myself. It creaked as it rose. When it reached its apex the hinge snapped, slamming down so hard that chunks of wood flew. Iona growled softly. I looked back at her, hand raised.

"Don't worry. I'm fine." She growled warningly, although I wasn't sure whether it was at me or the disintegrating ship.

I braced one hand on each side of the hole and dropped down. The ship groaned and shifted, but it didn't move far; it must have been shoved too far onto the rocks for my weight to make too much difference. Disintegrating wooden crates left shards everywhere, sharp pieces crunching under the soles of my boots. I stumbled over a large chunk and knelt, then jerked upright, swallowing hard.

"Iona, I could really use your help," I mumbled softly, stepping over the item. It was not, in fact, a chunk of wood as I had thought, but rather a pale white bone. An arm bone, if I wasn't mistaken. Completely stripped of flesh.

I tried not to see it, but there were others as well. Arms, legs, and crunched skulls, their lower jaws missing. The intelligent part of me insisted that I find a way out of the hold, jump on Iona's back, and never look back, doing my best to forget what I had seen here. That's what the smart part of me said, but it warred with my intense desire to see why there were so many bodies.

Their positions suggested that they had died protecting something.

I picked my way over the bones. Only one of the skeletons seemed intact, sitting upright in the corner. A tarnished silver ring with a red gem drooped on the left ring finger; I rubbed the ring around my middle finger in response, where my armor was held in place. A roll of yellowing parchment was clutched in the same hand. I brushed it with my fingers. I wanted to take it, but this was the perfect opportunity for a booby trap, as even I knew with my limited experience. I had to be careful.

I didn't move, searching the floor for any sort of wire, or any piece of the floor that looked different from the rest. I tested the boards with my feet before I moved. When nothing immediately killed me, I moved closer to the skeleton, angling my shoulders so that my body didn't block the little light filtering from above.

The boat creaked and I staggered a step as it shifted. Iona roared a warning. I nodded in agreement that it was time to leave and tugged on the map, then gently pried it from the skeleton's fingers.

A high pitched whistle was my only warning before an enormous arrow shot from the wall, punching through the opposite wall, whistling over my head as I dropped like a stone. The ship lurched and I yelped as I slid, scrambling for something to grab. The bones rolled under my fingers. I slammed against the far wall, the ship groaning; the impact punched my foot through the floorboards, up to my ankle in the frigid ocean water.

Iona roared, and her panic shot through our bond. Wooden shards rained down on my head as she ripped the boards of the deck free with powerful thrusts of her claws.

I couldn't decide whether covering my head or pulling my foot free was the more important task at hand, so I compromised by covering my head and hunkering down.

"Be careful!"

She growled and I conceded the point. Her claws tightened on my upper arms and pulled. My ankle protested, the bone grinding, then ripped free as the boards gave a similar protesting groan and then ripped free as well. Iona flapped mightily to drag me out of the hold. Her grip on my arms was tight as she wheeled away from the ship.

"You can put me down," I called up to her. She lowered her head between her forelegs to look at me and snorted. All I could feel from her was irritation. I sighed and tried to make myself more comfortable.

This time when Iona dropped me, I was ready. I tucked my arms and legs into a tight ball and rolled back to my feet in one fluid motion, something that had taken many falls and much practice to perfect. Iona paced, her tail whipping angrily; her deep growls rumbled through her chest as she bared her teeth at nothing. It sounded like she was grumbling to herself, and I bit my lip as I struggled not to laugh, because that wouldn't help her irritation any.

I sat down as close to the edge of the stone stack, the same one from the night before, as I could without being in danger of falling off. I carefully peeled off my boot. My ankle was red and slightly swollen, but it was no more than a few scratches. I swiped away the fresh beads of blood with my fingers and pulled my boot back on.

It had been hard to hold onto the parchment from the ship with my arms raised over my head, but I had managed. Iona was still pacing, so I carefully unrolled the parchment and laid it on the ground, placing my hands on the edges to keep it open.

I frowned at the map. "Iona, come here." She growled, but ceased her pacing to join me. Her head lowered over my shoulder as she sniffed it carefully. Her slitted amber eyes met mine. I retrieved my own map from my armor and spread it above the new map. The two were drastically different.

The new map, or new to me at least, showed one massive landmass, the rest of the parchment peppered with smaller islands. Notations in faded ink were legible on nearly every bit of the page not marked by some sort of landmass. There were no navigational markers, but there were plenty of drawings of sea monsters and other dangerous creatures.

On the other hand, my map showed no such large

landmass. So far I had spent most of my exploration time documenting the island that I had once called my home. It had taken us months of exhaustively flying over every inch of the island to document it on my map. I knew for a fact that my map wasn't wrong, which was why I was so perplexed by this ancient one.

I carefully lifted the parchment and turned it over, searching for any sort of date or identifying, such as the mapmaker's name, but there was none. I would have to study it further later. Right now, my blood was pumping too fast to stand still for long. I carefully folded both maps and placed them in the pocket of my skirt, then turned back to Iona.

"See? Worth it to explore the ship." As soon as the words were out of my mouth, I wanted to suck them back in. Iona's growls resumed and she paced to the edge of the stack. I edged to the other side and squinted. My eyes widened.

The ship we had left was in flames. I had thought it would sink, partially because I had put my foot through the deck and partly because Iona's weight had dislodged it from the position that had kept it from sinking to the bottom of the sea for years uncountable. The flames were an unearthly blue, a blue that sang to me of dangerous enchantments.

"Iona," I called. I could feel how she felt through our bond. True anger, not just irritation, and the cold blade of fear. I went to stand in front of her, placing my left hand gently on the side of her face. "Look at me." Her amber eyes met mine, her wings rising and falling in a bristling challenge.

"I'm sorry that I scared you. I wanted to explore, but I should have realized that it would upset you. I'm sorry."

I lowered my head, my hands still cradling her face. After a short hesitation, she lowered her head to press against my face. Her scales were cool against my skin. The growls slowed, and she offered me her back. I jumped up, then cleared my throat.

"Oh, and the ship is on fire." Scales clicked as she whipped her head around to look at me. I held my hands up, cringing slightly. "Sorry. Just thought you ought to know." I was extremely glad that I had been in the saddle before I had said anything, or I may have spent the next hour chasing her around this tiny little hunk of rock and trying not to get bitten. As it was, she was none too happy with me, not that I could blame her. She launched into the air with a dizzying series of twists and twirls, and I hunkered down with my hands gripping the straps at the front of the saddle.

Chapter Four

"More trees," I complained under my breath; Iona grumbled in response, smoke trailing from her nostrils. The air was calm and still, making us both feel lazy. Iona's wings beat only sporadically, spread wide to catch the air currents and glide. I drew as carefully as I could, the map balanced against the front of the saddle. There was so little wind that the page hardly stirred.

I squinted. Plenty of trees, yes, but a flash of stone. I pointed, leaning forward so that Iona could follow my finger to where I was pointing. "There. What's that?"

Her wings angled toward where I was pointing. She tucked her wings and pointed her muzzle down, drawing closer to the stone. These weren't natural formations, as I had assumed, but rather carved statues of dragons. I studied them quickly as Iona winged in slow circles. The statues were similar enough to be of the same dragon, but slight differences told me that wasn't the case. Different scales here; different eyes there. One was missing a claw, too large of a mistake to have been coincidental.

Iona swerved with a high cry of alarm as figures in dark clothing now filled the clearing below. Arrows flew and she pumped her wings to avoid them, struggling to gain enough altitude to escape. A large machine of some sort was wheeled below us and launched a net.

"Look out!" I yelled, flattening myself to the saddle.

With a mighty flap of her wings she made a valiant attempt to climb out of range; the net whistled through the air. The rope fibers caught her wing and neck, pinning her wing in place. We plummeted toward the earth, and I hugged the saddle for dear life, which was all I could do with my forearms pinned to the saddle.

The impact cracked my bones. Iona did her best to protect me but only managed to tuck slightly. I kicked out as our attackers rushed, leaping forward ro hold her muzzle in place. Smoke trailed from her slitted nostrils; her body shook with vicious snarls, her tail lashing as they tried to pin that as well.

"We mean you no harm," I said calmly, trying to convey sincerity, which was difficult without being able to move my hands.

Their masked faces showed no sign of fear. Even if we had meant them harm, with my hands tied and Iona's muzzle bound, it wouldn't have mattered. The leader said something in a low voice to a smaller fighter, who scampered away into the woods.

The silence grew tense. I had no idea what we were waiting for. I tried to casually work my hands free of the net; the leader noticed and slapped the back of my hand with the flat of his dagger, hard enough to sting but not hard enough to wound. I stopped moving.

Wings beat and I craned my neck to see the dragon above us. Silver claws flashed, and massive wings flared as he landed. Iona's head lifted, the net shifting. This dragon was purple like her, the only other one I had seen of the color. His scales were so dark as to be almost black with the same silver veins streaking through his wings. More importantly, seated in front of those wings was a rider, face obscured by a fierce black helmet. Not a wild dragon, then, but one with a rider.

A blade flashed as he dismounted and I went rigid.

The tip of his knife forced my chin up. Iona's snarls intensified. She struggled and I cried out as the net's cords cut deep into my forearms. The rider removed the blade and sliced through the net with one quick stroke. A few low words, and the fighters melted away. The rider climbed onto his dragon's back and motioned to the sky.

The message was clear: Follow us.

Iona swiveled to cast me an inquiring glance. I sighed.

"Not like we have much choice." She huffed in agreement and launched into the sky.

Both dragons tilted into a steep dive, wings flaring to land on a mountain plateau. I jumped out of the saddle, squaring off with the rider. Iona snarled and squared up with the larger dragon, who didn't rise to the challenge.

The other rider dismounted and removed his helmet.

Thick brown hair rippled over his shoulders. Clear green eyes shone in the sun. A thin scar on his cheekbone was pale white, stark against the rest of his skin. His lips were chapped like mine from too much time spent at high altitudes. I drew my own knife and held it angled across my body; I hadn't been able to reach it before, with the netting, and I made a mental note to make sure that I had more than one knife in case I couldn't reach one of them. The boy didn't draw his own weapon, but hung his helmet from the saddle.

"Who are you?" I snapped out immediately.

"Just give me a moment to explain."

"Quickly." Iona snarled to emphasize my point. "Before we lose our temper."

The darker male dragon offered his nose to Iona in greeting, then ripped it back hurriedly as she took a swipe with her gleaming claws. A clear warning.

"My name is Lochlan. I am as much a prisoner on this island as you are, and I am not your enemy."

I stared at him, resting my hand on Iona's shoulder.

Slowly I lowered my dagger, returning it to its sheath. The least I could do was hear him out. It could do no harm, and might even help in the long run. "What are you talking about? We aren't prisoners here," I said.

Iona shook her head, ears pinned, and I couldn't help but agree with her assessment. My statement had been purely bravado. As soon as we had flown over the statues I had felt strangely uneasy; the fact that we had been shot down had done nothing to dispel that anxiety. We had been shot down before, but always because the people feared a dragon and her rider. With Lochlan and his dragon here, there was no real reason for them to fear us, and thus no reason for them to shoot us down. Nothing about this situation made any sense.

"Those people who shot you down worship a *dragon goddess*. They believe that you and I are the goddess' chosen ones, and that our dragons are her gifts."

Iona peeled herself out from under my hand, pouncing toward the larger dragon like a playful kitten, which was the complete opposite of how she had been acting toward him a moment ago; even with our bond, I had no idea what had changed. I went rigid as the dragon growled, but it was playful; he took a half-hearted swipe at Iona and they hopped away.

I rolled my eyes.

"Some gift," I said. Then turned back to Lochlan, studying him.

He wore dark armor like mine with plates of thinly hammered metal that overlapped like dragon scales covering his chest. Black pants were tucked into dark boots. He was slender, built like the dragons we rode, like me. Or I like him, depending on who was older.

"How long have you been trapped here?" I asked.

Lochlan seated himself on a boulder, his long hair sliding as he raised his head to look at me. I chose another for myself and sat a few feet away, close enough to speak but far enough that I didn't feel threatened.

"A few months. I tried to leave a few times, but every time I did..." He made a vague gesture back the way we had come, clearly indicating being shot down. I winced sympathetically as he continued. "So we stayed. We have some freedom, and so we learned to accept our fate."

"So you're just going to let them trap you here?" I gawked at him.

Lochlan's eyes flashed. His dragon paused, tensing with his paw raised. "Do you think I'm any happier about this than you? Lochlore and I are just as used to flying free as you are, if not more so." He was standing over me, fists clenched.

Lochlore glanced up at the sound of his name. An interesting name, made even more so by its similarity to Lochlan's. It had been a fun adventure to choose Iona's name. She had already been an adolescent when we bonded, not fully grown by certainly full of her own opinions. If she hadn't liked the name, she had taken a swipe at my head with either her paw or her tail. And I had gotten good at ducking.

After a few days of suggestions, the swipes had become slower and more good-natured, like she was finally realizing that I had no idea what I was doing. She had finally settled on the name Iona, right before knocking me flat on my back with her tail.

I softened my voice when I next spoke. "I'm sorry. I understand. I shouldn't have snapped before I knew what was going on."

I was wary of him because he had threatened us, but if what he said was true, then he was only doing what he had to do to protect his dragon. I couldn't fault him for that, even if I didn't appreciate a knife being held to my throat in the course of keeping up his act.

He nodded slowly. "I didn't know how you would react. I can't imagine that I would have felt any differently," he murmured.

"So what are we going to do? We both want to get out of here, and we've both been shot down. Tell me what you've learned so far."

Iona and Loch had tired themselves out. Iona flung herself down and I grunted as her head hit my lap. I stroked her long neck gently as she curled her tail around in front of us. Lochlore was more dignified; he sat behind Lochlan and slightly to his left, then wrapped his paw around Lochlan's chest and pulled him back against his scaled chest. Lochlan flailed briefly, then settled.

"Honestly, I don't know much about the situation. For the first couple of weeks we just kept trying to escape." He smiled crookedly. "That doesn't exactly inspire trust with the locals. That's when they told me that I was the chosen warrior of the dragon goddess. Or rather, they wanted to know why I was trying to leave if I was one."

I grinned just as crookedly. "I'm sure that was an interesting conversation." I fiddled nervously with the ring around my middle finger, adjusting my armor. The sun was beginning to set, and as much as I wanted to think that Iona and I would be able to just fly out of here under cover of night, I had a bad feeling it wouldn't be that easy.

"So how do they keep you here?"

He grimaced. Although he couldn't see his rider's expression, Lore growled in agreement.

"They have sentries scattered on every peak, always within eyesight of the next. Everytime we tried to fly out, someone shot us down." Loch rubbed the side of his neck, where a pale white scar slashed diagonally. When he noticed that I was looking, he smiled wryly. "Last time they shot us down, we panicked and one of Lore's claws scratched my neck."

Lore whined softly and shoved his head under Loch's arm, eyes apologetic. Loch stroked his scaled nose gently and I felt a pang of recognition. That was what I looked like when I petted Iona.

My emotion must have trickled down the bond, because Iona jerked her head from my lap, her ears pointed straight up. I closed my eyes as she pressed her face to mine, the scales cool on my forehead. She hummed softly.

Loch allowed us our moment of affection before he spoke again. "We're under guard all the time, even while we sleep."

I frowned. Guards were a problem. I was an explorer, not a fighter, hence my armor; it was for my protection.

Cool liquid kissed my skin and I raised my head. A thick fog was settling over the island, the heavy dampness depositing tiny water droplets on my exposed hands and face. Iona's tongue flicked out experimentally.

Loch raised his eyes to the sky. For one, he was expressive when he wasn't wearing his helmet, and for another, my limited experience with the inhabitants of this island had told me that they were people to be wary of. Perhaps that was why he always looked to the sky, to ensure that none of the others were near us, although watching the ground might be a better option.

I tugged the top of Iona's saddle and she rose to her feet with a discontent grumble. I swung into the saddle and Loch did the same on his dragon. I touched the helmet hanging from my saddle, then changed my mind.

"Let's go."

The dragons lurched into the darkening sky. Iona and I were used to flying alone, and it showed. Iona's wing clipped Lore's shoulder; we plunged downward and I let out a startled yell. Iona curled up as much as she could. The impact jolted me free of the saddle and I rolled, crashing against one of the boulders in the middle of the clearing. I groaned softly. The day's bruises were going to be epic. First the impact of being shot down and now this.

I sat up slowly, wrapping my arm around my stomach. Loch was sprawled half over Lore's saddle, one foot still in the stirrup. He sat up slowly, wincing. Iona uncoiled herself, peeling her wing out from under her chest and paws, shaking it to check that it was still functioning properly. Satisfied that it was, she snaked her head under my arm and helped me to my feet. I climbed into the saddle with shaking legs.

"Let's try this again," I mumbled, and Loch nodded. This time, we all paid more attention when the dragons took to the air. I hugged the saddle and made minute adjustments to help Iona balance. The two dragons hovered in place as they found their rhythm. Wings pumping, Iona and I followed Lochlore, but to what...we didn't know.

Chapter Five

The wind whistled in my ears as we soared, my silver braid whipping against my back. It was too loud to speak, especially since Loch and Lore were a wingbeat ahead of us on the left. Iona seemed content to hang here, wings beating occasionally.

The island was heavily forested; dark shapes darted in the tall gray trees, but we were too far up to make out anything distinct. Hills rose into the sky. Tall mountain peaks lowered to flat plateaus. We flew over them all, and soon a village came into view.

Loch pointed down; I dismounted as soon as we touched down, resting my hand on Iona's amethyst neck. She bristled as all eyes turned to us. Loch's shoulders tensed, his strides quickening as he led us toward the stone door in the hill.

No one spoke, but all eyes watched. Children paused in their energetic games to stare at the dragons. Iona's tail swished in the leaves, her wings held out to the sides and half-raised; anxiety and warm anger prowled through the bond. Otherwise her wings would be folded tightly against her sides, but I sensed her readiness to be in the air once again.

Two guards stood beside the stone door, one on each side. The butts of their spears left deep imprints in the ground, the tips gleaming darkly in the last rays of the setting sun. At Loch's nod, they pushed the heavy door open. It had seemed small at first, but as we stepped closer, I saw that it was wide and tall enough to admit the dragons. Lore led the way, followed by Loch.

Iona's claws shredded the dirt and she reared back, refusing to enter the cramped space. I went rigid as the guards lowered their spears. Iona snarled, lips curling back from her teeth.

My mind darted around in circles as I searched for a solution. As much as I agreed with her not wanting to be trapped in a dark space guarded by angry men with pointy weapons, I also didn't want her to have to eat someone to get out of this situation. Dragons were strong, fierce creatures, even one as small and slender as Iona. Their scales were hard as iron and practically fireproof. Her rider, on the other hand, was a lot easier to damage. Those spears could shred right through my armor.

Loch's eyes were wide with horror. I bent next to Iona, trying to calm her. "Calm down, girl. It's just for a little while."

She huffed but squeezed through the doorway, her tail brushing my ankle as I followed. The door closed behind us with a heavy, final thud. I swallowed hard.

The space was larger than I expected, an arched stone roof that would have allowed the dragons to stand on their hind legs with room to spare. A round hole in the roof admitted soft silver rays of moonlight. A spark of hope leapt in my chest, only to be dashed when I realized that it was too small for the dragons. Loch or I could climb right through it, but that didn't matter; we couldn't escape the island on our own, and that was if we had been willing to leave our dragons behind, which was never going to happen. We were days from the nearest village that I knew of. We couldn't exactly swim there.

Just below the hole was a deep pool of water, the stone surrounding it etched with runes. Deep lines were carved into the floor, an odd sensation beneath my boots. Iona put her nose to the runes and tracked them around the room, tail swishing. The water in the pool was a deep green, which I eyed doubtfully.

As questionable as the water seemed, I was more concerned with the stone altar in the center of the floor. Iron chains were tossed onto the surface; dark, suspicious looking stains dripped down the side and onto the floor. Iona growled at it. I had to agree.

"So what is this place? A prison?"

He grinned without humor. "Not exactly."

I followed his eyes to the rear of the cave. I stepped closer, putting my hand out so that I didn't bump into Iona, who was still sniffing. The statue was of a woman, or so it seemed. Massive wings, carved from glistening black stone, jutted from her shoulders, so very much like Iona's that I turned to look at her. Curling horns like a ram's drooped over the woman's shoulders. Dark shapes like scales covered her face and arms. Most alarming of all, the runes at the base of the statue had been chiseled away. Any goddess that even her own people wouldn't name was not someone that I wanted to associate with.

"This is a temple," I realized. Iona had climbed onto the altar, her tail hanging over the side, and my anxiety spiked. "Iona, get down from there." She leapt down and prowled toward me with a growl, but her heart wasn't in it. She was as skittish as I. If we had been trapped in a cave, I would have understood. Being trapped in the temple of a forsaken goddess with a strange rider and his dragon, the only other like my own that I had ever seen, was entirely another matter.

Loch nodded. "This was the first place they brought me after they shot us down. That first time was rough."

I arched my brows. "Rougher than any other time being shot down?"

Lore huffed softly; it took me a moment to recognize it as a laugh. Loch shoved his dragon's shoulder lightly, but it was done with the same affection as every other action.

"Yes, actually. When they shot us down, it knocked me free and I landed away from Lore. They were ready to kill me before Lore protected me."

Lore nosed Loch's shoulder and Iona did the same with me, nosing her head under my arm. "Well, at least they didn't kill you. Instead they've held you captive for months."

He made a face. "The gods have strange blessings."

I leaned against Iona, glancing at the strange statue once more. "Do you know the dragon goddess' name?"

He shook his head. "They won't say. No one will tell me her name or anything about her. Only that she is the goddess of dragons and that since I'm a dragon rider, I must be one of her chosen few." He gestured at me, clearly including me in the description.

"That's alarming."

"Along with everything else about this place," Loch grumbled. Lore sprawled on his side with one wing raised; Loch sat, curling up against Lore's side. He tugged at the sleeves of his armor.

I stared at him, somewhat horrified at the thought of sleeping here. "Do we sleep here? In the temple?"

He smirked, his thick brown hair sliding back from his face as he looked at me. "Why? Suddenly you're worried about offending the goddess that you don't believe in?"

I held up a finger to correct him. "I never said that I didn't believe in her, only that I didn't know of her. Besides, I'm not eager to offend anyone's goddess."

Iona stretched out, curling her tail around her legs, and I looked for a good place to sleep. The idea of sleeping in a stone crypt made me ill. We were used to sleeping under the starry sky, lulled to slumber by the whispers of the ocean and waking to the rising sun. Hard dirt and frigid stone were not the same.

I followed Loch's eyes to the altar. It was the highest flat point in the chamber and the only one that was shaped even remotely like a sleeping surface. I eyed the hard stone, the chains coiled as if they were waiting for their next victim, and shuddered violently.

"I don't want to give them any ideas."

I lowered myself to the ground and curled up next to Iona. Her paw curled around my stomach and both of us looked to the sky.

Chapter Six

"Do you always sleep that way?"

Iona scales dug into my stomach, the edge of her bony wing in my hip. I slid off and rolled over, glaring at Loch. He seemed wide awake. I hated him for it.

"Yes, I do," I informed him. Iona's long teeth flashed as she yawned. The light falling through the hole in the ceiling filtered through her wings, cascading onto the floor near her tail. My tailbone jolted on the floor as she nudged me off. I glared and she rumbled in response.

"Why?" Loch asked. "It can't be very comfortable."

"Why do you sleep the way you do?" I shot back. "I just do."

Loch held up his hands in surrender. "As you wish. Once you're ready, we can go into town to break our fast."

I made a face at him and climbed to my feet, stepping

over Iona's paws to stare doubtfully into the water of the fountain. I had slept in my armor, just like I always did. I unwound my braid and let my silver hair fall around my shoulders, dipping the tips of my fingers into the water to help with combing through the tangles. Loch watched curiously; Lore was not so reserved. He sniffed my hair with interest and I flipped the strands forward so that he had better access. Iona was grumbling about her dislike of how close he was to me with her anxiety filtering through the bond.

Loch rolled his eyes at Lore's antics, but even that didn't hide his curiosity. "Has your hair always been like that?" he asked. I arched a brow at him with a smirk. I knew he meant the odd color, an old maid's hair on a girl no older than he was, but I was going to make him say it. It was a small enough payback for him threatening me the day before. He gestured at his own hair, then sighed. "Has your hair always been that color?"

I shook my head, pausing in braiding so that it wasn't crooked. "My hair was brown when I was born, just like yours. My mother always says that my foolish antics turned it prematurely silver."

Stone grated as the door of the temple was pushed open. Two guards gestured with their spears. Loch went first, with Lore crowding his heels. The guards' spears clattered on the stone and Iona snarled. I rubbed the arch of her neck gently, squinting in the light of the sun. It hadn't fully risen yet, but after spending the night in the darkness of the cave that admitted only a sliver of moonlight, the brightness was blinding.

Once outside I reached to climb onto Iona's back. One of the guards reached out and hooked the butt of his spear between my ankles, giving it a sharp yank. I tumbled to the ground.

"What are you doing?" I snapped, rubbing my arm. I wasn't entirely sure which part of me hurt the most, since most of the day had been one jolt after another, so my arm would have to do. Iona growled in confirmation. The guards stared impassively, their spears leveled at my chest as I rose slowly.

Loch stepped between us. "She didn't know. We don't have a problem."

Iona was snarling as she leaned into my hand; I leaned against her, sliding my feet to keep her behind me.

"I don't know about what?" The guards turned away and I turned on Loch. "What did we do that got them so riled up?"

"They have strange ideas about riding dragons."

"Strange ideas?" I asked, trying to curb my irritation, which Iona was clearly feeling as well. Lore sniffed her neck; her paw flashed out, smacking the side of his muzzle reproachfully. Luckily her claws were sheathed, so it produced a satisfying thwack but no real damage.

"They fear dragons as emissaries of the dragon

goddess. They see us as emissaries as well, since we ride them."

The guards prodded us forward with their spears, but I was too focused on Loch's words to mind. He continued to speak as we trekked toward the village, visible only by the plume of dark smoke in the distance.

"I understand that, but what does that have to do with the guards not allowing me to ride Iona?"

"We can only ride during certain times of the day. We can only fly in the evenings, but they won't even let us ride our dragons until after the morning meal."

"I'll have to get used to walking," I said glumly.

Iona loped ahead, pouncing on Lore's back. They twisted away and I rolled my eyes. The guards retreated to a small distance, leaving Loch and I walking together in companionable silence.

I glanced at him out of the corner of my eye, taking in his armor once more. It made sense that one would think that we were together. Our armor was very similar, black leather with the scales of our dragons on top, although Lore's scales were a darker purple than Iona's. My armor had shoulder pads, the places where I hid my maps and drawings, while Loch's did not. We both wore dark boots and had helmets hooked to our saddles; the way the dragons were rolling around right now, wrestling over a massive stick that might more aptly be called a log, we'd have to make sure that the helmets weren't lost in the thick undergrowth.

All eyes in the village turned to us. I folded my arms across my stomach, gripping my elbows with my long fingers as I shrank back into myself. Loch slowed his steps to fall back to my side. My anxiety must have reached Iona, because she gave Lore one last good smack on the nose with her paw and bounded back to me.

Loch touched my hand gently, guiding me toward the center of the village. A massive pot hung over a roaring fire, suspended on a stand by short chains. Two women stirred the liquid inside with long wooden spoons. Children ceased their playing when they saw the dragons, sneaking closer and then squealing away when Iona sniffed at them. She had only the barest experience with children, having only met my younger siblings a few times; I saw them as often as I could, but Iona rarely accompanied me. I wasn't sure whether or not she liked children; she may not have known herself. All I felt from her was a soft curiosity mingled with anxiety, which could have been the children or simply the village itself. We were still on edge, but if what Loch said was to be believed, we couldn't risk the people of this island thinking that we were trying to escape. For now, we were stuck here.

Iona's tongue flicked out as she tasted the air, following her nose toward some sort of enormous fish roasting over a smaller fire. One of the women tending the spiked monstrosity patted Iona's nose, gently pushing her away from the tall, spiked fins on its back.

"Careful, dragon. The spikes are poisonous." As we watched, a drop of yellow liquid dripped from the tip of one of the spikes, dribbling down the silver fish's side. The woman thrust a small glass vial over the flames to catch the bead, thick leather gloves protecting her hands from the heat.

I leaned closer to the fish, the heat from the flames warming me, heating the leather of my armor. I was tempted to draw the fish, but I didn't dare. They didn't know how much I knew; for now, it was safer for me to pretend to be a simpleton, or at the very least aloof. Shows of knowledge often started a cycle of questions that I couldn't, or wouldn't, answer.

"What kind of fish is it?" I asked curiously. One or two questions wasn't going to draw any attention, so I figured I was safe enough with that.

"We call it a Spikefish," the woman explained. "Its venom is a powerful poison. It causes dizziness, nausea, and is even used as a sleep aid. In correct doses, it can even make someone appear to have joined the gods."

I swallowed hard. A fish like that was a dangerous fish. It was dangerous to even be near this creature, let alone be stealing its poison. I drew my knife from the sheath on my wrist. Both Loch and the woman went rigid, but I only poked the tip into the fish's scaly hide, then raised the tip to study it. There was no poison on the blade, which was odd. Perhaps it was only on the spikes? If so, that was a very inefficient delivery system. All a predator had to do was take a chunk out of the side or the bottom, or even grab it by the tail...

I shook myself. Not the time, nor was it very important to the situation at hand.

"Can you eat it?" I asked. My growling stomach told me that *that* was the question that I should be asking.

The woman laughed, although she was still eyeing my knife. I hurriedly jabbed it back into its sheath, nearly stabbing myself in the arm in the process; cheeks flushed, I rearranged my armor, tugging on the ring around my middle finger. She laughed, although I didn't feel as though it was in a mean spirit.

"Yes, you can eat it, dragon rider. Are you hungry?"

"Yes, Lady." I hesitated, unsure of what to call her.

She laughed again and motioned for us to sit down on the logs around the fire. Loch and I sat together, the shoulders of our armor clicking. I scooted away; Iona made a soft huh-huh-huh sound that I took as a laugh, which only got louder when I nearly scooted off the log. Loch reached out to steady me; my eyes dropped to his hand. His armor led to a ring on his middle finger, but only on his right hand. His left hand had a leather gauntlet; the hilt of a knife jutted near the heel of his hand.

The woman returned with two slabs of wood, on

which steaming pieces of fish and small berries sat. She handed one to each of us and sat next to us, flicking her gloves over her knee. I picked up a piece of fish and hissed as it scalded my fingertips, licking them to ease the burn once I had dropped the fish back onto the plank; learning from my mistake, Loch munched on a berry instead.

"Thank you."

She nodded, watching the flames. "I'm Avren. I've gotten to know Lochlan and Lochlore. I look forward to getting to know you as well." Lore nuzzled her shoulder and was rewarded with a piece of fish, which may have been the reason that he did it in the first place. He snapped it out of the air with a clatter of teeth.

I balanced the slab on my knees and reached to grab Avren's forearm. Her brows rose as the leather of my armor creaked in her grip when she returned the gesture.

"I'm Asta. My dragon is Iona." I hesitated, unsure if I had already said too much. I wasn't sure how a people who worshiped a fearsome dragon goddess would take me calling Iona "mine." They might find it an insult and decide that they needed to free her from me.

"It is a great pleasure to meet you, Asta. And where are you from?"

I was not going to answer that. As friendly as Avren seemed, I couldn't forget that her people were holding my dragon and I hostage. The only person I would even consider trusting here was Loch, and even that was still up for debate. After being their prisoner for months, I couldn't be sure that he hadn't come around to their way of thinking. Even the strongest minds could be changed with enough time and I had no way of knowing how strong Loch's mind was.

"Far from here," I said evasively. "Iona and I explore long distances."

"Do you miss home?" Loch asked suddenly.

I blinked in surprise, then swallowed. The odd question prompted me to answer with honesty.

"Some parts. My family, my friends, everywhere I knew as a child." I took a few more bites of fish to avoid saying anything else, but Avren wasn't finished with her questions.

"Does that mean that you joined the service of the goddess as a youth then? Not as a child?"

Finished with my meal I set the wood aside and wrapped my arms around my knees. Strangely enough, what I said next didn't feel like a lie. It felt right.

"I was always a strange child, so I'm not surprised that a dragon became my closest friend. Iona and I were both injured fighting another dragon. That must have been her call to choose me and my call to join the goddess."

Most of that had been the truth. Iona and I had been injured fighting a dragon and that had been the beginning of our friendship. The only thing that hadn't been true had been about joining the service of the dragon goddess.

Any goddess that was spoken of only in harsh whispers and was unnamed even to her closest followers wasn't one that I was eager to encounter.

Avren had paled when I mentioned fighting another dragon. Perhaps I should have been concerned with offending her delicate sensibilities. But she didn't seem offended; if anything, she seemed scared.

"You fought another dragon?"

I nodded slowly. She lurched to her feet, hands shaking as she took our plates. I watched her walk away, clearly in a hurry. No one else approached us, so Loch and I sat calmly. Iona slipped her head under my arm, her scales rasping on my armor. I rested my hand on the side of her face, not stroking, just enjoying one another's company.

"Does your family know?" Loch asked suddenly.

I frowned at him, puzzled. "Know about what?" I assumed that he was referring to some part of the story that I had told Avren, although I wasn't sure which part.

He nodded toward Iona, whose ears pricked at the attention. "About how you met your dragon."

"Yes. She picked a fight with some of the dragons near my village and lost. I found her while she was injured and took care of her. Or tried to, anyway."

"It didn't work out too well," he said, more an observation than a question. Nevertheless, I nodded.

"She picks fights that she can't win." I wrestled gently

with her to prove my point. She munched on the shoulder of my armor, adding another set of tooth gouges. A purple dragon was painted on my upper arm. It had taken much trial and error to find the right purple to match Iona's scales, as perfectly as I could manage. It had taken even longer for me to decide that I was satisfied with the drawing. My drawing skills were decent, enough to record the things that I saw or the ideas that I had. I was picky about the way that I looked, or at least when it came to my armor. It had to be perfect before I put it on.

"Why do you think she likes to fight so much?" Loch was feeding Lore the pieces of his fish, munching on the berries himself.

I shrugged. I had never given it much thought, to be honest. It was just the way that she had always been, or at least as long as I had known her, and questioning why would not change anything. "She's small. Maybe she feels the need to prove something."

"Not like you." His eyes met mine. We were both nearly as slight as our dragons, a full head shorter than the guards that had kept us trapped in the temple or even the women around the fire.

"I still feel like I have something to prove. I just don't fight to do my proving." Unconsciously I rested my hand on the spot that hid my maps. My parents had always thought that I was strange, but they hadn't fully given up on me doing something worthwhile until I had bonded with Iona. Dragons weren't outright hated at home, but they were deeply mistrusted, as elsewhere in my village. Now I wasn't welcome in their presence anymore.

I stood, glancing at the fires around us. No one else was eating; all of the adults were bustling about, tending the fires or cleaning up the dishes. I padded over to where Avren was piling more wood onto the flames beneath the Spikefish. The two women next to her watched us warily.

"What's happening, Avren?" I asked.

She looked at Loch before she answered, but wouldn't make eye contact with me.

'We have preparations to make. Be on your way."

I frowned. Clearly they were trying to get rid of us, but I was shocked that she was so short with us. Just minutes ago we had been having a friendly conversation, but now she was acting as if she had never met me. Loch glanced at me, equally confused.

"Be on your way," Avren repeated more sharply. Her eyes flicked away, then back, then away again. I didn't spend much time around other human beings, but even I could sense that she was warning us about something. I bowed my head, motioning for Loch to lead the way.

"As you wish."

Lore bounced into the trees; Iona swept her wing over my head and I ducked when I heard the telltale whoosh, narrowly missing the branch that Lore's tail snapped back. It smacked back and hit Loch full in the chest.

I winced in sympathy. "That looked like it hurt." I patted Iona's flank as thanks for the warning. Her tail brushed the leaves aside as she dashed after Lore.

"It did," Loch agreed. We chose a spot overlooking the village, a flat plateau that gave us a view of everything happening below. The children had been sent to play in one corner, under the watchful eye of a woman building a pyre. Two men were digging two deep, round holes in the soft dirt, adding to a tall pile next to them. Two logs with bases roughly the same size lay a short distance away, carefully being stripped of their bark with knives.

I frowned. "Any idea what's happening?"

To me, it looked like preparations for something, perhaps a ceremony of some sort. The care they were giving each and every task told me that it was an uncommon occurrence; if whatever they were preparing for happened more often, then they wouldn't have cared so much.

Loch shook his head. "They've been preparing for weeks. The past few days, the preparations have doubled, like they're running out of time."

"Perhaps it's some sort of gathering or fair," I theorized. Groups of men were struggling to move massive logs down the hill, where more men waited to chop them into more manageable chunks. Realization struck.

"Iona, come on."

She was neck deep in a log and peeled herself out of it

to paddle after me. The men glanced up, cringing when they saw her. I held my hands up to show that I meant them no harm.

"Would you like some help?" I motioned at Iona, then rolled my eyes and picked a sliver of bark from her muzzle, her eyes rolling back to their proper positions. "We can help you with the logs."

Loch picked his way down the hill to join us, his cheeks flushed as he panted for breath. "We can help too."

The men glanced at one another and I waited patiently for their answer. If any of them would allow us to help with the preparations for whatever gathering or event would seem to be taking place, it would do great things to earn their trust.

I decided to risk taking it one step further, in order to make their decision easier. I chose my words carefully. "The goddess looks fondly on those who honor her. It allows her to be closer to you when we provide aid."

Loch joined in smoothly. I hadn't known him long, but I did have to be impressed by how seamlessly he had picked up my tactic.

"It would be our honor, and the goddess' wish." That seemed to make the decision easier for them, although they still seemed suspicious. Perhaps it was because they knew it would take them days of hard labor to accomplish the task. With the help of two dragons, even dragons as small as ours, the work would go much more quickly.

"Aye. If that's what you want."

Now the hard part. I directed Iona into the air, hovering over the pile of logs. She grasped the top in one of her claws and lifted it, shoulders straining to handle the weight. She flew it down to the pile the other men were chopping, flaring her wings in order to balance. Lore repeated the process.

Now that we had the basic mechanics down, all that was left was to work out the finer points. The next time it was Iona's turn to take a log, she gripped the log in her claws and I lifted it from beneath, helping her to raise it into the air. With me helping her from below, there was less weight on her shoulders and wings. Loch climbed up next to me and we both helped Lore.

With all of us working together, the dragons made short work of the pile. As soon as we were finished, the workers sent us on our way once more.

'We can help with something else," Loch offered.

Heads shook. Once more we wandered into the wilderness, the dragons padding ahead of us. Iona's ears pricked. Within a few steps I could hear a soft rush of water.

I sighed as I followed Iona. Loch glanced at me, brushing his hair out of his eyes.

"What's the matter?"

I pointed to the dragons ahead of us. Lore was nosing in every tree and bush which, while perhaps not being the most dignified approach, did at least not make him look like a fool. Iona, on the other hand, was a very different story. She was chasing her tail, tangling her wings in the bushes, and just generally making a nuisance of herself. She wasn't normally this strange, but perhaps only spending time with me for long stretches of time had stunted her somehow. Perhaps she needed more time with her own kind, not that either of us had great experiences with other dragons. Just another problem to worry about.

"Iona isn't normally this..." I searched for a word to express my concerns. "Strange. Something about being here is making her foolish."

Loch patted Lore's tail, deftly avoiding it when it swept back at him. "It is a lonely life. It does them good to spend time with other dragons."

I caught his green eyes. "And it does us no harm to spend time with another dragon rider, right?"

We laughed as both of the dragons plunged into the stream, although I had to wince soon after, because all of our equipment was still strapped to their saddles. It would take hours to dry out, but it was too late now. Iona swished her tail experimentally; once she understood how it felt in the water, she flipped the broad, oar-like tail and flung a wave of water. Too late I realized who it was directed at, and all I could do was stand there and be doused. Water dripped from my chin, pasting my silver hair to my face. I spat out a mouthful of water, although it was far less than I might have taken in had I not been prepared, and used my free hand to wipe my face.

"Thank you, Iona. I appreciate that."

Loch threw his head back and laughed, shaking his thick brown hair so that he could splash water droplets on me, not that it mattered much because of how wet I already was. He had been standing close enough that he had gotten just as wet as I had. He bent to remove his boots and the outer pieces of his armor, leaving only the base layer. He waded into the water, turning back to look at me. I cocked my eyebrow, but he just shrugged, not the slightest bit concerned about my judgment.

"I'm already wet. I may as well have some fun." He dove into the water, pouncing on Lore's tail. I rolled my eyes but stripped down as well, diving into the water after them.

Utterly spent after more than an hour in the water, I climbed up onto the shore and sprawled on my back. Loch did the same, curling up on his side. His long fingers grasped a loose strand of my silver hair, winding it.

"You have such striking looks," he said finally. In my opinion, he was quite the looker himself. His dark brown hair was so wet that it was nearly black, curling around his ears. He had a split in his full lower lip, likely the result of his latest run in with the guards during an escape attempt. Droplets of water clung to the thick lashes obscuring his pale green eyes. To me the most attractive thing about him was that he didn't seem to notice how eye-catching his own looks were. Or perhaps he had spent so much time surrounded by the enemy, with only his dragon for company, that he wasn't sure how to act around people his own age.

"Thank you."

I flushed, gently untangling my hair from his grip but softening the blow by untying my braid, stroking my fingers gently through the wet locks. It would dry more quickly this way anyway; the only reason that I had decided to braid it once I was in the water was because it was in my way, and there was no reason not to let it breathe for a moment now that I was on dry land.

I wrung out my hair, then laid back next to Loch. Iona wedged her foreleg under my head as a pillow, curling around me and placing her head on my stomach. I stroked her head, laughing as she nudged the pocket in my armor where my drawings were hidden. I wasn't ready to show him my map yet, but I didn't mind him seeing the drawings. With her message delivered, she dumped me unceremoniously, her tail flicking.

"All right. Go on then." I nudged her away, then changed my mind and caught the strap of her saddle to stop her. The first time that she had gone into the water I hadn't known she was going to do it. If I was going to send her back into the water, then I was at least going to take off all of our gear. Two dousings in one day might be more than it could handle. I pulled off her tack, then nudged her toward the water. She flung herself into the depths and came up with a fish flopping in her mouth. Lore leapt in to join her.

I reached into the hidden pocket to withdraw a clean sheet of paper. My fingers brushed the slick surface of the oilcloth that lined it. The oilcloth was specially designed to keep water or any other elements from damaging my precious works. I dried my hands as best as I could, then laid out the page on the ground and dug through my bag for my pen.

Loch sat up, learning forward with interest. "What is it?"

In answer, I leaned forward and sketched a quick outline of the statue of the dragon goddess, ending with the massive wings. Loch watched me draw, then held his hand out, dark eyebrows raised in silent question. I handed it over.

"Fascinating," he murmured, turning it over in his fingers to study it. "How did you make it?"

I cocked an eyebrow, surprised that he assumed that I had made it. When most people saw me, they saw a scrawny explorer, not strong or smart enough to do anything that would be of benefit to my own clan. And yet here was Loch, who I had met yesterday and knew not at all, who had naturally assumed that I was smart enough to create this item that he looked at with such wonder. It was a refreshing change.

"Are they hard to make?" Loch asked when I failed to answer him.

I shrugged, cheeks flushed. "I need some specific supplies, but I could make more if given enough time."

He handed it back and I went back to sketching. I darkened and shaded the picture of the goddess, nervous about drawing in front of him, then began work on one of the two of them. I pulled it back into my lap so that he couldn't see it, no matter how hard he tried to peek over my shoulder.

The wind picked up, my silver hair whipping my cheek. The drawing of the ship blew from the pile and Loch snatched it from the air, carefully smoothing the edges. It felt like a lifetime ago, although it had only been a few days. I flushed under the scrutiny. That drawing was much better than the one of the dragon goddess, partly because I hadn't been rushed and partly because I had been relaxed, without someone looking over my shoulder to make me nervous. Iona didn't count.

"This is amazing."

I glanced up, meeting his eyes. The green shore in the sun, so pale it was almost translucent. He offered a shy smile, which I returned.

"Thank you."

His long fingers tapped on his knees as he seemed to

war with himself, then reached into his armor and withdrew a piece of thick parchment. I gathered up my drawings and tucked them away, again careful not to reveal my map. My eyes widened as Loch revealed one of his own.

The edges were soft with use, crinkling under my fingers as I leaned forward to study it more closely. This map was nothing like mine, nor like anything I had ever seen before. The land masses that were marked were different from the ones on mine. I had confidence that my map was correct, which meant that he and I had been exploring different areas. Stylized depictions of sea monsters poked here and there from the water. Tiny markings in a language I couldn't decipher marked each of the creatures.

"It's an interesting map." I considered showing him mine, but his own reluctance suggested I should wait.

He nodded, carefully folding it. "This was my task. I was sent from my homeland to explore and report back."

I frowned. "You were sent?" Being an explorer wasn't so much a task for me, but rather a product of the fact that I didn't have a choice. It was an odd concept, to think that he had been sent as a way to help his people and was not hated for it. "Why you? Are there no other dragon riders where you are from?"

Loch's shoulders went rigid. I searched his eyes for some clue as to why the sudden change had occurred, but he glanced away, refusing to meet my eyes.

"I dare not say. I should never have said anything in the first place. Once this is over, we will never see one another again. You don't know me."

Anger spiked in my chest. Here I had thought that we were building trust, but I meant nothing to him at all. I gathered up the last of my drawings and stood. Iona poked from the water, water dripping from her pointed ears; sensing my anger and frustration, she prowled onto the bank, snarling a warning at Loch as she passed. That brought Lore out of the water, legs stiff as he raised his wings to cast a massive shadow. I didn't look at either of them as I threw on the saddle, hands shaking as I tightened the buckles. I jumped into the saddle.

"If that's how you feel," I said coldly. Iona leapt into the air, her tail snapping toward them both, Loch's hair falling back from his face as the gust reached him. His lips moved, but I looked away. I didn't want to hear anything that he had to say. He was right about one thing: as soon as we escaped, we would never see one another again. The sooner we both realized that, the better.

Chapter Seven

Being trapped on an island with nowhere to go was bad enough. Being trapped on a small island with nowhere to go was even worse. I wanted to get away from Loch just as much as I wanted to avoid the village, but I didn't know my way around, so I chose the lesser of two evils. Iona and I landed on a small hill overlooking the village with a view so that we could see the others coming from any direction. Once more I laid out my map, then flipped it over.

    Drawn on the back, in as much detail as possible, were the phases of the moon. I had drawn them as carefully and precisely as I could. It had taken years of careful study to reach this level. It allowed me to plan my travels and track what day it was. It wouldn't have been important, except for one thing.

    Every three months I returned home. My mother and

father did not want to see me, but I had younger siblings who did. Our standing date was for every three months; they would sneak out at night to meet me, and I would spend as much time with them as I could before we had to go our separate ways.

My trips served two purposes. First and foremost was the obvious: a chance to see my siblings. Secondly, I took a different route home each time, carefully marking the path on my map. In the case of an emergency, I knew which path would take me home the fastest. Besides, there was no telling what interesting things I might find on the way.

Iona dropped something and I jerked, letting out a startled yelp as the thing in my lap moved. The rabbit trembled in my lap, its downy gray fur pasted to its body with Iona's saliva. I stroked it gently. Slowly the shivers eased.

"Thank you, Iona." She nuzzled my shoulder gently, purring in response. While I was perplexed by her choice in how to cheer me up, I had to admit that it was working. Iona settled with her tail coiled around us both, occasionally nosing the rabbit. Shifting the rabbit to my left thigh, I traced the phases of the moon with my finger.

Even if I took the fastest flight path I knew of to get home, I would only just make it in time for my meeting with my siblings. If I didn't leave in the next few days, I wouldn't make it at all. The situation had become much more urgent.

Iona growled a warning just as Lore lowered himself to the ground, allowing Loch to dismount. The rabbit, able to stand one dragon, just couldn't manage two; it hopped out of my lap and bounced away, one hind paw thwacking my thigh as it went. Loch watched it go, perplexed. He shook himself.

I folded my map and tucked it away, standing to face Loch. He lowered his head, long brown hair sliding into his face. He was picking at the ring around his middle finger to adjust his armor.

"I'm sorry," he burst out. "I was so excited to show you my map, but then I thought about what the consequences would be if anyone ever found out." He sighed gustily. "I don't want that for either of us. You have to understand."

Irritation rose in my chest, tempered by curiosity and the realization that most of my anger was in fact anxiety about going home. It wasn't Loch's fault that I might not make it home in time to see my siblings. He didn't know anything about me.

It wouldn't be fair to take my nervousness out on him, even if he had hurt my feelings earlier.

"So what? Are you here to apologize, or to insult me again?"

"An apology. And to check on you. I wanted to see how you were faring with everything."

"I assume you mean our newfound captivity and not your insult?" I checked, cocking an eyebrow. He flushed.

"Yes."

"In that case, the biggest problem I have is that I need to get home." I could see that he was going to start sympathizing with me for being sick for home. I had to make him understand. "I don't just want to leave this island, I *need* to. I have an important meeting to make."

His dark eyebrows arched, but he didn't comment. "How soon?"

"Soon enough that if I don't leave this forsaken island in the next few weeks, then I won't make it."

"Is it your family?"

I blinked at him, shocked that he had put it together so quickly. "Yes. But not my parents."

He sat next to me. Iona seemed unsure if I was still angry; I smiled and nodded at her, allowing calm to flow down the bond. She leapt to her feet and licked my face, my hair sticking to her tongue. I rolled my eyes as she rumbled a laugh.

"You just had to ruin a good moment, didn't you?"

She and Lore bounded away, still in sight but not close enough to interfere with our conversation.

"Why not your parents?"

I hesitated, unsure how to answer, or even if I should

answer at all. Loch seemed to be giving me the option, which meant that I had to. I would feel guilty if I didn't. "There are dragons where I'm from, but not like them." I nodded toward Iona and Lore, who were trying to tunnel under a log for some unknown reason. I rolled my eyes.

"They are enormous blue creatures that move slowly and think even slower. My people have made an uneasy alliance with them. They help us with our tasks and we allow them to hunt on our land."

"And your parents don't agree with that," Loch guessed. I shook my head grimly.

"My parents still remember the days when the dragons took what they wanted and gave nothing back."

I tugged on the ring around my middle finger. Adjusting my armor was my nervous habit. Even though I knew my armor looked fine, it made me feel better to have something to do with my hands.

"The day I bonded with Iona, I tried to tell them about her. They didn't take it very well." My mouth twisted. That was rather an understatement. "They told me that if I left with a dragon, I shouldn't come back. And as far as they know, I never have. Every three months I meet my siblings under the cover of night."

Loch nodded in understanding. "So that's why you're so desperate to get off this island."

"Yes. I'm afraid if I don't make it home in time, my siblings will be found out, and I might never see them again." I swallowed hard. I hadn't even known that I was afraid of that until I had said it aloud. Now that I had, I wished I hadn't.

To my surprise, Loch rested his hand gently on my knee. The dragons looked up, ears pricked. I stared into his clear green eyes.

"I'm glad that you shared this with me, even after I couldn't give you the same trust." He offered me a hand to help me to my feet. Iona nosed her head under my arm, wrapping her tail around my ankles. "And I promise that I will do everything I can to get you off this island."

"We can do this. We are dragon riders and we can do this."

I looked at him quietly. I hadn't trusted him before, but telling him about my family had opened a door between us. If we were going to escape, we had to trust our dragons and ourselves. If we did that, then nothing could stop us.

Chapter Eight

Now that we had decided to escape in earnest, the only problem that remained was how to go about it. Or rather, that was the biggest problem, one that branched out into many smaller issues. We knew relatively little about how we were being kept here, and there was also the matter of the preparations. It could have been something as simple as a festival, but given how determined the villagers were to keep us from learning anything about it, I doubted it was anything so gentle. Until we knew for sure, we had to treat it like a threat. Given the rapid increase in the activity to prepare, we had to assume that the danger grew with each passing day.

We had to escape soon or we might never have a chance.

Loch and I talked through every scenario that we

could think of, pointing out any flaws that we could see. It was rather disheartening; every plan we could manage had at least one glaring flaw. Finally we decided on a simpler approach. I would sneak out of the temple through the hole in the ceiling and lure the guards away. Loch and the dragons would meet me on the top of the hill nearest to the village and we'd take off from there.

We had consulted our maps, Loch next to me and me in private, and found an island that would be able to provide us with food and water for the journey ahead. Now all we had to do was escape. Which was the hard part.

I picked anxiously at my armor, glancing up toward the silver moonlight filtering through the hole in the ceiling. We were waiting for the moon to fall before we made our escape, plenty of time for the guards to tire. It was awful trying to wait, not helped by the fact that a blood red cast had crept over the moon as I watched.

"That can't be a good omen," I murmured. Loch hesitated in his pacing, swinging his head to follow my pointing finger. He swallowed hard and nodded in agreement, but neither of us spoke any more on the subject. Perhaps we were afraid to say anything that would change our minds, or shatter our already strained morale. If nothing else, it was a dangerous game to play, and both of us decided that it was best not to tempt fate.

Finally the time came to make our move. Loch and I

were both on the small side, as slender and rangy as our dragons. In order for me to be able to reach the hole in the ceiling, we had to climb onto the altar. Loch boosted me up, his hands braced against my boots as he held me steady. I could feel his arms shaking with the strain, but he didn't once complain. Placing my hands on either side of the round opening, I hauled myself up and out; my hips scraped briefly but slid through the hole with little resistance. I thanked the gods that I was small. I had always been slight, but even more so now that I had bonded with Iona.

Not only had bonding with Iona stunted my growth, it had made other changes as well. For months after we had formed the bond, my bones had been weak, filling me with deep aches; even the slightest of jolts had broken the tender bones. I had a theory that it was the bond's way of making me lighter to make riding easier on Iona. If my bones had become hollow like a bird's, it would explain the temporary weakness, as well as why my growth had slowed nearly to a stop. I was still growing and had reached a respectable height, but I would never be overly large. That came in handy in situations like this.

I poked my head out and glanced around. Everything in me told me to run, to avoid the guards, but I forced myself to step into their line of sight and whistle softly. They turned, eyes widening when they saw that I was no longer in the temple. Their spears clattered as they shot into motion; I took off, bolting toward the hill where I would meet the others. I didn't have to outrun them for long, just long enough to get to Iona. I was counting on them not to call out to the rest of the village, since they would want to fix their mistake and have us back where we belonged before anyone found out that we had escaped.

I flung myself into the saddle; Iona's leg muscles tensed as she launched upward, a dizzying sudden rush of air. My stomach lurched. Loch leaned over Lore's back. This time, there was no clash of wings; the dragons spiraled tightly, in each other's space but spaced perfectly so that they didn't touch.

The guards had changed their mind; they sprinted toward the village, spears clanging as they shouted. Flames flickered as torches were quickly lit, but we were already at the edge of the island. Cautiously I looked back, then raised my arms to the sky and let out a fierce whoop. Loch smiled as he joined in, a smile that dropped immediately.

Massive wings blocked out the darkness of the blood red moon. This dragon was easily the size of both Lore and Iona combined, with flesh to spare. Its armored stomach was covered with pale scars. Spikes covered its neck and tail, which was tipped with a heavy growth of bone, also studded with spikes. Four long claws jutted from each of its front paws, but there were only three on the hind paws. Not that it mattered, because any of the claws looked like they could be the end of all of us.

The dragon's icy blue eyes narrowed to slits as it noticed us. Iona slowed to a stop, wings beating slowly as she hovered. Lore took position beside us. His mouth opened, a bright blue glow building behind his teeth. The subtle hiss built in Iona's throat as she did the same. I placed one hand on her neck; one ear flicked back to listen.

"Don't fire first. Maybe if it doesn't see us as a threat it won't attack." The best that she would have been able to do was blow smoke at it, but that might be the only thing that would set it off. There was no way to know, so it was best not to do anything at all.

That was the hope, but it turned out to be unfounded.

Nostrils flared, the dragon opened its mouth to snarl, an eerie crackling sound filling the air between us. Iona couldn't breathe fire, so I couldn't be sure that was what it was about to do, but there was enough in the sound and the rippling glow in its throat to make me nervous.

With a huge bellow, a gout of flame spurted from between its teeth. Iona dove, tucking her wings to plummet beneath the orange fire, so close that the blue at its heart seared into my eyes. I blinked and shook my head. Iona and Loch dove and twisted; I was only vaguely aware of the dark shape. I couldn't warn Iona as the dragon's massive paw swung forward, because I didn't see it until it was far too late. Iona twisted frantically, taking the blow on her side and wing. Loch's tail clipped her, and both dragons plunged toward the rocks.

The blow was crushing. I hugged as close to Iona's back as I could, but the impact from the blow was so strong that it ripped me from the saddle. Sharp stones dug into my stomach and sides as I rolled toward the edge of the cliff. I clawed for anything to stop my slide, but I couldn't see well enough to grasp anything. Unable to arrest my fall, the last thing I heard was Iona's anguished screech and the hungry roar of the waves below me. I plummeted into the water, what little of my sight that had returned fading to black.

Chapter Nine

Cool scales brushed my face. Everything hurt, pain radiating from my very bones. Grit covered my eyes. I raised my shaking hands to the skin under my eyes, scraping away the crust with my short nails. I blinked slowly and squinted.

Iona licked my face, sticking her tongue out in disgust when she encountered the salt from the sea; I could taste it on my lips, stinging in the cuts. Droplets of water were cool on my skin. I tried to sit up, then winced and leaned back. My head was pillowed on Iona's forelegs, her tail coiled around us both. I reached once more to rub my face, then paused when I felt the coolness of scales on my skin. This time, I realized that it was not in a place that Iona could possibly have been, so I had no idea why there were scales there.

This time I did sit up, although I winced as I did so. My hair was pasted to my face; I ran my fingers through it quickly, flipping the soaked locks away from my face so that I could see better, then lowered my hand, eyes widening.

Pale purple scales covered my right wrist. The leather of my armor was torn, stained with dark blood and salt. I probed it with my fingertips. The skin around it was skin just as it should have been. The scales were the odd part.

Thinking that they were Iona's scales that had somehow become stuck, perhaps with the ocean water, I tried to peel them off. When they didn't budge, I wedged my fingers beneath them and yanked. Iona licked them, raising her golden eyes to mine. Realization dawned slowly.

"Oh," I said softly. The scales weren't going to come off. I didn't know how or why, but somehow Iona had healed my injuries, which must have been severe enough to cause her concern. I did a quick patdown to check for other injuries, but my wrist was the only part of me with scales. Everywhere else felt tender and bruised, but whatever injury of my wrist had concerned Iona enough to use magic to heal me hadn't extended to the other parts. I was only partially glad. On the one hand, I didn't want to be entirely covered with scales, but I also wouldn't have minded not feeling like every part and parcel of my body had been pounded with rocks.

My eyes widened and I scrambled to my feet, swaying as the blood rushed to my head and black spots danced at the edges of my vision; it had returned to normal and had been that way since I had woken up, which I was grateful for. If I had been injured badly enough that Iona had healed me, thus giving me scales, there was no telling how badly Loch had been injured. I didn't dare call too much attention to us in case the villagers were still nearby and looking for us, so I had to do this quietly.

"Loch?" I called softly, glancing around for any sign of either him or Lore. Iona heaved herself to her feet, head hanging low with exhaustion. Her wings and tail dragged in the dirt. I stroked her head gently in concern; her muzzle nudged me in response. Healing me after the fall must have taken all of her energy. I had been more worried about Loch than my own dragon, and I felt awful. I promised myself that from now on, we would come first.

"You can stay here," I offered, stepping to the side so that I was looking into her eyes. Her head snapped back and forth on her long neck in a clear denial. I sighed. I couldn't actually be angry with her for being stubborn when I was the same way myself. It frustrated me beyond belief.

"Loch!" I called again.

Iona swerved around me, her nose raised into the air like a hunting hound's. I followed her quietly, unwilling to break her concentration. Soon enough we caught sight of

Lore, who raised his head at our approach. Relief flooded my chest as I saw Loch's dark waves against his dragon's chest.

I knelt in front of Lore; Iona sat next to my back, curling her tail gently around my ankles in silent support. Lore hesitated, then opened his paws, easing Loch's head down to the rock. When we had fallen off the cliff, I hadn't known what was beneath us, since we hadn't exactly had time to explore; I had expected a splattering death on the rocks below. Instead, judging by the salt on my face and how wet I was, I must have fallen into the sea, and a part of it that was deep enough to allow us to fall into it without being completely shattered by the impact. It was only by the blessing of the gods that I had been mostly uninjured, and I sent up a silent prayer that the favor would be extended to Loch as well.

For a terrifying moment it seemed as if he'd died. Panic made my heartbeat surge and warm tears pricked at my eyes, my throat closing in panic, but I struggled to contain the tears. I placed my hand on his chest, sitting back on my heels as I felt the steady beats of his heart under my palm, his chest rising and falling. His face was turned away from me, his long brown hair obscuring it, so I placed my hand under his chin and gently turned him toward me.

I gasped, the ring on my middle finger touching my lip as I placed my hands over my mouth. Blue-green scales, unlike any I had ever seen before, covered the skin of his high cheekbone and curved around his eye. I touched it gently, and his eyes opened.

His green eyes met mine, a shade paler than the scales next to them. His hand rose, and for a breathless moment I thought that he was going to cup my face as I had his. Instead he tucked my silver hair behind my ear.

"For a moment I thought you were a goddess, here to take me to the afterlife."

I sat back as he leaned up, wincing. "And now?"

"I'm not sure. I think you're better than a goddess. I'll take a dragon rider any day."

I flushed, scrambling backward so quickly that I tripped over Iona's tail and fell on my own. "I think you hit your head."

He winced and touched his face. I tensed as I waited for him to discover the scales on his face; his fingers skimmed over it without pausing. I breathed easier, but in the back of my mind I wondered what I would do when he discovered them. He eventually had to. Every moment in the meantime would make it harder to explain why I hadn't told him that he had the appearance of a dragon, or at least partially. It didn't detract from his looks, but it was startling at first glance. I had to tell him.

"Actually, I know you hit your head." I reached up to brush my hair back from my face and Loch's eyes dropped to my wrist, to the gleam of scales not hidden by my armor. He took my wrist gently.

"What happened?" He frowned, squinting. "Are these Iona's scales?"

I coughed, unsure of how to phrase what I wanted to say. "I can see how you would think that, but no. Apparently, they're mine."

Loch's eyes widened with a look verging on panic. "I don't understand."

"When we fell, we must have been injured. Our dragons healed us."

He glanced down at his hands. His armor was intact. Mine was irritating me; the sooner I could repair it, the better I would feel.

"But I feel fine."

I hesitated. "Your scales aren't on your wrist." And that was part of the problem. If they had been on his hands, or anywhere else I could have shown him, it would have been easier for him to understand. Realization struck and I leapt up, digging through Iona's saddlebags until my fingers closed around a small object. It was a mirror shard, part of a mirror that I had shattered before I left home. The edges were filed so that they weren't jagged enough to cut., so I had no reason to fear that Loch would cut himself when I passed it to him. He angled it so that he could see his face, then dropped it in shock.

"I have scales."

"Yes."

"I have scales," he repeated in a tone of shock. I could see that he was winding up for another one, so I took the shard and sat down in front of him. The dragons curled around us, forming a never ending circle of wings and scales.

"We both do," I pointed out. My connection to Iona felt stronger than ever. Right now she was anxious and sad. I had been so worried about the scales that I hadn't considered how we had gotten them. All the work, all the struggle, and we had nothing to show for it. We were still stuck on this island, with no more idea of how to escape than we'd had before. Less of one, in fact.

Anger spiked through the bond. Iona rose, snarling.

"What is it, Lore?" Loch asked in concern. Both of our dragons were growling as they prowled around us. My back bumped into Loch's. All I could feel was anger and fear, with an undertone of sadness.

"They thought they were going to lose us," I realized. The anger was pierced with something like agreement, which meant that I was right. Iona's teeth closed around my hand, although they didn't pierce the skin. I raised my other hand to her scaly cheek and spoke into her ear.

"I'm sorry," I whispered.

"Isn't that sweet?" A net descended over Iona and rough hands dragged me away. Loch and I both struggled, but we were no match for the men holding us, and they quickly stripped us of our knives and anything else that might even vaguely be considered a weapon. "Take them back to the camp." Avren braced her foot against the net pinning Iona and Lore to the ground. "And take them separately."

I sighed darkly as I tugged on the chains binding us to the altar in the temple. The altar had only been made for one prisoner, so things were a little tight. Loch and I were both chained to the altar, his wrists in the set that the chains were intended for and mine in the set that was meant for the ankles. Things were close on the hard stone, simply because there wasn't enough chain for us to move any further away. I wrapped my arms around my legs, the chains cool even through my clothing.

Avren reached through the bars of the cage to touch Iona's bound muzzle. Gone was the gentle, inquisitive woman who had fed us by the fireside. This was a woman hard as steel, one who ruled her people like the goddess they so feared.

"Avren, what's going on?"

She chuckled, seating herself in the chair that one of her cronies had brought her. "Asta, Loch, I must say how impressed I am at how close you managed to get to the edge of the island."

"Honestly, so am I," Loch said, and I nodded in agreement. "A dragon like that is the best perimeter guard that someone could ask for."

"It's not a perimeter guard. That creature is the curse of the dragon goddess. It eats and kills as it wishes."

"Well, I'm sorry about that, but I still don't understand what that has to do with us." I rattled the chains to illustrate my point. "Especially now."

"Well, the plan was to sacrifice you at the rise of the blood moon." Her tone and phrasing suggested that was no longer the plan; she pointed through the hole in the ceiling to illustrate why. The moon was slender and silver once more, with no trace of the rusty darkness from before.

"That's why the pyres and all the wood," Loch said. Avren nodded. "What about the dragons?" I asked. "Did you really think that they would just stand by and watch as you roasted their riders alive?"

"I didn't know how close you all were. As far as I knew, you were keeping them captive somehow." She unfolded herself from the chair and strode toward us, gripping Loch's chin and turning his face so that she could see his scales. "Now I see that isn't true."

Fury rose in my chest. In the cage, smoke trickled from Iona's nostrils as she snarled, but the leather band around her muzzle prevented her from lashing out with any efficacy. I hopped off the altar and shifted forward until I was stopped by the chains. Avren returned to her chair, although I had the feeling that she was humoring me.

"I see now that you truly are chosen by the goddess."

I fought the urge to laugh hysterically. All it had taken for them to believe our lie was a failed escape attempt and gaining scales. If I had known that from the beginning... I still didn't know what I would have done.

"So what does that mean for us?" I asked coolly. Standing here in chains while the person who was holding us against our will called us the chosen of a goddess felt like a cosmic joke, like the gods themselves were laughing at us.

"It means that we look to you for a solution to the problem with the dragon."

This time Loch laughed before I could, muffling it with his hand over his mouth. He gasped before he spoke.

"Because we did so well with that before." He motioned to his face and I shifted my hand to cover the ones on my wrist, trying to act nonchalant. As far as they knew, I didn't have any scales. I didn't know why it mattered, but I knew enough to know that any information I had that they didn't could be used to our advantage.

Avren's face tightened. "Be that as it may, we still look to you. I'm sure that you can think of something. I'll leave you to pray on it."

Chapter Ten

I lifted my arm, glaring balefully at the chain that dangled from the manacle on my wrist.

"I understand what these are for now."

Loch arched a dark brow, green eyes glittering in the soft light. "And you didn't before?"

I rolled my eyes, punching his arm lightly. His armor was just as hard as mine; neither of us were hurt, unless the slight ache in my knuckles counted. The punch had been more out of frustration than anything.

We had been sitting here for hours, both of us curled up on the stone altar, huddled close for comfort. Loch's hand rested on my shoulder; I derived as much comfort from that as I did from the bond with Iona. I could feel that she wasn't injured, just angry and scared. A thick leather band prevented her from opening her jaws. Thick iron chains were coiled through the bars, additional insurance, besides the lock, that the door wouldn't open.

Every half an hour, one of Avren's lackies poked their head in and asked if we had a plan yet. Each time we'd heard them coming and managed to look like they were praying by the time they opened the door, but it was only a matter of time before they grew tired of waiting. We had to come up with something, and quickly. All of our lives depended on it.

I rested my hand lightly on my map, then withdrew the whole stack of papers. Loch's eyes flicked through the drawings, then widened as I spread the map on the stone between us. I rearranged the chains across my lap and sat in silence as Loch studied it. His long fingers traced my drawings slowly, following the lines of my home and all of the small islands that I had mapped; this island was by far the largest I had ever even attempted to map, but due to its inhabitants, I was happy to let it remain a secret. If it wasn't, then more people would come here, and that was the last thing that I wanted. I felt surprisingly vulnerable showing him my map, although it was only fair. He had shown me his map but not his home. I was showing him both.

"Asta, this is amazing," he breathed. I flushed and picked at my ring, my fingers dropping to the scales below it. If I didn't repair it soon, I would have a new bad habit on my hands.

"Thank you. When I left home with Iona, this map was my escape. It's been my labor, my way of seeing the world, ever since."

Loch reached across the map to squeeze my hand gently.

"I'm sorry that you were sent away from your home. I was as well, but I know I can always come home." I squeezed his hand in return, looking longingly at the cage in the corner. Loch and Lore were relatively new additions to my life, new friends that had been the briefest of enemies. Iona had been my constant companion for years. The bond was still strong between us, but I would have preferred physical contact at this moment.

Loch seemed to have the same idea. He climbed off the altar and paced toward the cage, going as far as the chains would allow him. He sighed and sat down; Iona backed away, allowing Lore to press his face to the bars. The few feet that separated them couldn't have been any farther.

The stone door of the temple scraped open, propelled by two guards. Avren stopped on the threshold and crossed her arms. It looked like our time had run out, and I scrambled for any semblance of a plan to feed to her.

"What is your plan?"

My mind flashed back to the map that Loch had shown me. There had been a larger map that he had shown me first, but I had also seen a smaller map of the island itself. A series of tunnels dead ended into a cave with a hole in the roof, just like this place. I had no idea how big it was or the exact orientation of the tunnels in relation to the cave, but an insane plan began to form.

"We'll need a few more hours to finalize it."

"I'd like to hear what you have so far."

Loch glanced back at me with his eyebrows raised, like he wanted to know that too. Anxiety spiked from Iona and my eyes flicked in her direction, then met Avren's.

"There are a series of tunnels at the interior of the island that lead to a large cave. We plan to lure the dragon into the tunnels and trap it there."

Avren nodded; both she and Loch looked impressed. She motioned for the guards to remove our chains. I rushed to stand in front of the cage, only standing back to allow them to unlock it. I pulled the muzzle off Iona's face, my shaking hands struggling to undo the buckles.

"I guess we're going now," Loch mumbled. We followed the dragons out of the temple and took to the sky.

Since we hadn't had time to truly plan out the details, we spent our time in the air working out at least the rough outline of a plan. We kept a wary eye out for the dragon, but even so, it was the village inhabitants who spotted it first. Their screams and pointing fingers pointed us toward the massive dragon.

"My turn." I urged Iona toward it, intentionally

winging as close as I could manage. Massive wings beat in pursuit. Iona plunged into the entrance of the tunnels and the chase began.

I thanked the gods for how small Iona was. Her wings brushed the sides of the tunnel, leaving just enough room for her to maneuver; that was part of the reason that she and I had taken on this part of the plan rather than Loch and Lore, since there was no telling how difficult it would be for them to take the tight turns in the tunnels. The dragon behind us was not so lucky, but rather crashed against the walls and collapsed the tunnel behind us, stone crumbling. I ducked against Iona's back, flattening myself against her scales as pebbles rained on my head and shoulders.

"There," I called, pointing toward the tunnel veering to the right. Iona tucked her wings and rolled. The massive dragon's teeth crunched onto stone, a short burst of flame dissipating against the wall. The cave appeared ahead, which meant that we were running out of room to take our shot. Iona's hind legs dropped to propel us upward, the one mistake that she made.

The Goddess Bane's claws gouged deeply into Iona's hindquarters and my right leg along with it. I cried out as hot blood trickled down my leg. I drew my knife, which had been returned, twisted around in the saddle, and flung it at the dragon's eye. Of course it didn't connect; I didn't want to hurt it, just to get it to back off for a moment.

Iona's hind legs dropped once more, muscles bunching as she launched herself into the air and through the hole in the ceiling.

The stone cracked but held, the enormous dragon trapped in the caverns below. Iona plummeted to the ground and I was thrown free, bouncing on the hard ground. I limped to Iona's side, veering around Loch as Lore landed.

"Iona, are you okay?"

She twisted to look. Deep scratches covered her hindquarters, releasing a slow trickle of blood. She nuzzled my arm, but Loch was staring at me. Or rather, at my lower leg. I could feel the blood slowing.

"Asta, you're bleeding."

I waved away his concern to look back at Iona. Already the cuts were no longer bleeding, so perhaps they weren't as deep as I had thought. Lore was sniffing at my injured leg. Loch nudged him away, his green eyes going wide.

"What?" I asked, glancing down. My own eyes widened. More scales had appeared on my leg, scabbing over the injured part and dulling the pain to a fiery itch. Lore sneezed, looking pleased with himself, then turned to Iona's wounds. Soon enough her wounds were healed as well, the scales indistinguishable from the ones that had been ripped away.Some of those scales had been shed; inspired, I set about digging through my saddlebags for a needle, then used the scales to repair the tears in my armor. Loch watched, mouth twitching in amusement.

"Well done." He passed me one of Lore's scales, the last one that I needed to finish. I added it, then glanced back at the hole in the ground that dropped into the tunnel below.

"Now it's time to figure out what to do with that."

Chapter Eleven

I pointed Avren toward the ground, secretly hoping the Goddess Bane would flame and singe off her eyebrows. She stayed well back, clearly having the same thought after having seen the gouts of flame.

"The goddess told you that she would like you to worship it, in order to become even closer to her. It is her vessel."

This was what Loch and I had agreed on. We had trapped the dragon as much for our safety as for everyone else's, but since neither of us could bear to hurt it, it would have to stay trapped. This way, the people of the village could transfer their zealotry onto something that would survive it. At least, I hoped so.

"The goddess has shown us our next task."

"We have work to do elsewhere," Loch said seriously, bowing his head in false piety.

Avren nodded, bowing her head. "I understand. We are sad as to how events took place, and hope that you will consider coming back to grace us with your presence."

I nodded as I climbed into the saddle, waving as we took flight. We flew quickly toward the island that we had planned to escape to, flinging myself down as soon as we reached it. Iona sniffled the back of my neck.

"Absolutely not," I said fervently as I sat up. "I am never going back to that island."

"Agreed." Loch's tiny handwriting marked a warning on his map, one that I copied onto my own. Our maps were very different, but we were both similar in our pursuits. It could only benefit the both of us if we worked together, but I wasn't exactly sure how to broach the subject.

"I know we didn't trust each other with our maps at first, but I think we can help each other."

"What do you have in mind?" The dragons were playing near the edge of the cliff, but I didn't look away from Loch, trying to configure my expression to portray earnestness. I was fairly certain that the dragons could manage not to maim each other while we spoke for a few moments, and even if they did fall off the side of the island, they could fly. It wouldn't be time to worry unless Loch or I took a tumble.

"Every few months we come back here to make copies of our maps and check in with where the differences are. We'll be able to cover double the ground."

I could see him weighing his options, trying to decide if he trusted me or not. He held out his hand, which I shook.

"Deal. And in return, you help me find more like them." He nodded toward the dragons. I knew what he meant. Our dragons were the only ones that I had ever seen that looked like this. If there were more like them, we would find them. It was just one of the many things that I wanted to discover. I was eager to learn more with Iona by my side, and maybe some new friends too.

Epilogue

The woman smiled fondly, staring down at the reflection of the two young Dragon Speakers. They had no idea how intertwined their destinies truly were, especially considering that they had only just met one another. They had always been destined for great things, that much she had known from the start. After all, the girl had been born with the gift of speaking to dragons, and the fact that her silver hair had grown in at such a young age was only more testament to the fact that she would do great things someday. The boy had been born in a place that insisted upon conformity, and his lack of it, because of the fact that he could speak to dragons, had been the reason that he was sent away. Of course they had tried to say that it was simply because of his age and his ability to do things that no one else could do, but it wasn't difficult for any of them to realize that the poor boy was being exiled because of a talent that he had been born with, one that he couldn't help anymore than they could help their pale eyes or their fierce smiles.

Although his silver hair hadn't grown in like the girl's, the old woman had seen visions of the future where his long locks glittered like the moon on a frosted lake, so she was confident that such things might take time, but they would happen. But their adventures were not yet over, so there was plenty of time yet for the two young Speakers to grow into their destinies with their dragons. Time enough yet.

Book 2: Mistakes at the Hearth

Thank you for reading and I hope you liked it enough to leave a review! It really helps us authors out, and I'd super appreciate it.

The adventures continue in Book 2 of the Dragon Speaker Chronicles, Mistakes at the Hearth. One click now!

Also by Julie C. Kramer

SERIES BOOKS

The Science of Dragons

The Journey of Dragons

The Vigilante's Magic (The Vigilante's Magic Book 1)

The Vigilante's Darkness (The Vigilante's Magic Book 2)

The Vigilante's Sidekick (The Vigilante's Magic Book 3)

STANDALONES

Death and Other Misfortunes

Reporting to the Red Duchess

A Force of Thunderbirds

Dark Vessel

Champion of the Gods

Nostra

Motorcycles and Magic

Saga of a Fallen Valkyrie

The Stars In Every Sky

Shadows and Secrets

The Hellhound's Fiery Kiss

Of Curses and Scandals

Aerie of the Gryphons

Crystal Dark

Kings and Queens of War

Made in the USA
Columbia, SC
01 February 2025